Waves of Suspense

OTHER BOOKS FROM THE
HOUSTON WRITERS GUILD

Tides of Possibility

Edited by K.J. Russell

Published by SkipJack Publishing

Featuring more than two dozen pieces, "Tides of Possibility" is a proudly independent anthology presenting some of the most distinct rising voices in the genre. A new generation of science fiction is beginning, and the Houston Writers Guild has brought their words to print. The first in a series of anthologies from the Guild, it was produced using funds faithfully pledges by local readers.

Tides of Impossibility

Edited by K.J. Russell and C. Stuart Hardwick

Published by SkipJack Publishing

A proudly independent fantasy anthology, the Houston Writers Guild presents sixteen short stories: fables, sword and sorcery, and urban fantasy. These bold visions of the impossible will take you to worlds both very distant and closer than you'll believe. The second in a series of anthologies from the Guild, it was produced using funds faithfully pledges by local readers.

WAVES OF SUSPENSE

A Mystery Anthology
by the
Houston Writers Guild Press

Edited by Elizabeth Ann Domino

WAVES OF SUSPENSE
Copyright © 2015 Houston Writers Guild

Cover illustration by Verstandt Shelton
Interior design by David Welling

Houston Writers Guild Press
PO Box 42255
Houston TX 77242
www.houstonwritersguild.org

Ordering Information:
Quantity sales. Special discounts are available on quantity purchases by corporations, associations, and others. For details, contact the publisher at the address above.
Orders by U.S. trade bookstores and wholesalers. Please contact Houston Writers Guild Press at houstonwritersguild.org.

Printed in the United States of America

Publisher's Cataloging-in-Publication data
Waves of Suspense / Houston Writers Guild
p. cm.
ISBN 978-0-9969824-0-5

First Edition

— ⚬— CONTENTS —⚬—

—ᴍᴍ— FOREWORD —ᴍᴍ—

Elizabeth Ann Domino

I AM A FIRM BELIEVER that every person has a book inside them. Locked somewhere deep within the recesses of their brain, nestled in their soul, there lies a story waiting to be told.

Each individual's journey to write their story, their book, is personal and unique and utterly confusing. A Mad-Hatter attempt to connect the dots between what we know and what we create.

Words waiting to be woven, these stories range from flights of fantastical fairies, to comical anecdotes of charming cynicism, to poetic tales of paternal resentment. Sometimes they are nothing more than lyrical stanzas, scribbled randomness or bound journals of *War and Peace* proportions.

You have one. I have one. We all have one.

Some may be award winning-bestsellers while others appear as dog-eared board books or coffee table residents.

Others are lucky if they make it past the back of the toilet.

When I started my own journey I was apprehensive because I didn't think I had anything worth sharing. Who wanted to read anything I found the nerve to write? I had no penchant for character development, plots or worlds of other realms and dimensions. And half the things I thought and said weren't PG, much less PC.

I like to think of my story, my book as bathroom reading material. Not quite a bestseller or even fit for public, but something worth reading to pass the time. A fast-paced trashy bodice ripper speckled with colorful language, colorful women, it was a scathing semi-autobiographical look on life. With maybe a flashy sexy cover. The type you find next to the Raisinettes at CVS. Not quite Jackie Collins, but not *National Enquirer* trash either. I was not ashamed to think it. I was just too ashamed to write it.

Then I was introduced to this amazing community of writers through members of the Houston Writers Guild, and my book, my story found its way out. They held the key that unlocked that door.

I was fortunate enough to be surrounded by a number of people who enjoy reading anywhere and everywhere.

My relationship and involvement with the HWG has managed to outlast my first marriage and allowed me room to grow exponentially as a writer and as a person. It also allowed the thoughts racing through my head to come to fruition.

I am indebted to my colleagues and fellow community for the blood, sweat, tears, and toilet paper I have had the pleasure of using during my journey.

And that journey has brought me here. I am honored to bring you the first anthology from the Houston Writers Guild Press and invite you to read the stories from of our authors, share in the words they found within themselves.

And I encourage you to read this book everywhere. Not just in the bathroom.

—ᴂ— LUSCIOUS —ᴂ—

Teresa Trent

"OKAY CAROLYN, just grab that section on the corner and rip it off," Denny Elliot said as he held another piece of the ugly wallpaper. With a great effort Denny and his wife of twenty years pulled at the paper, and the mustard yellow sunflowers came off in one gigantic piece.

"Good work, getting that much wallpaper off at once is unheard of. Usually you have to take it off inch by inch," Denny said, amazed at the large piece he held in his hand.

Denny Elliot, a history professor and his wife Carolyn, a corporate manager, had lived in campus housing for most of their married life. It was fine for the two of them, never having had any children. Still, the dream of having their own home never seemed to fade away.

Denny would drive past the two story, brick home at 2445 Gossamer Street each time he made his weekly trip to the dry cleaners. Something about it pulled him in as if it were calling out to him a seductive silky voice. Beckoning to him. When the for sale sign went up in the yard, he pulled his car over and gazed into the windows. The house needed a little work, but it was set back from the road. In this house there would be no loud music or the familiar whiff of a freshly lit joint drifting out of the sociology professor's town home.

Denny and Caroline were much more conservative than the fellow professors who surrounded them in faculty housing. Probably the most objectionable thing Denny had ever done was collecting historic firearms, a big no-no in a liberal anti-gun community. He began imagining what it would be like to live away from the college and have a life outside academic life.

His wife Carolyn knew what that was like. She had worked at Martin Industries for almost a decade, although some of the people there were just as much of a pain as Denny's coworkers. Still though, she was able to spend the day away from the people he worked with. He rose around them, went to work with them, and then went home to a dwelling that shared a wall with them. He knew it was silly to move away from the college. The housing they were provided by the school was a bargain, and they had been able to save quite a hefty retirement fund over the years. It was like throwing away money. But still, even with all of that logical reasoning, something about the house was too much to pass up. Denny and Carolyn made an offer. A month later they moved out of their cramped two bedroom townhouse and into the house he had dreamed about, located at one 2445 Gossamer Street.

After mounting Denny's antique gun collection above the fireplace, the couple realized the rest of the house was in desperate need of redecorating. Most of the wallpaper, paneling and paint had been done somewhere in the Seventies. Goldenrod kitchen appliances, a frog-green tub, and the worst of all, those giant yellow flowers adorning the dining room wall. It was atrocious and just too much to bear. Had it ever looked good with a table and chairs in there?

"Oh my God," Carolyn said, pushing a strand of her shoulder length light-blond hair behind an ear. "What is that?"

Denny looked up at the wall expecting to see another layer of wallpaper, instead there was a mural painted across the expanse of the wall.

"It's a woman." It was indeed a buxom woman stretched out seductively on a couch, holding up a glass of champagne. She had a cigarette in the other hand and wore a low-cut, tight-clad dress with luxuriant red velvet folds that revealed a generous amount of bosom hanging out.

Seeing just the edge of some sort of lettering, Denny pulled off the remaining paper near the floor. There was a quote written in neat block letters.

ENJOY LIFE

BE THE PERSON YOU WERE MEANT TO BE

Denny started laughing, "Dang, Carolyn. We had some kind of a hoochi-koochie girl under our wallpaper."

Carolyn looked into the eyes of the woman in the painting. There was something about the two dark orbs. Something that seemed to pull her in. Denny became quiet as he too stared at the visage of the bare-breasted vixen. The doorbell rang behind them making Carolyn jump.

"Hopefully, that's the wallpaper I ordered, so we can cover it up," she said.

"Yes, not a minute too soon," Denny agreed still staring at the painting. The outlines of her body were not well drawn, and her face was almost cartoonish. She was the poster girl for hedonistic living. Was this garish woman the person the artist was meant to be, Denny wondered?

"Guess what," Carolyn said, returning to the room. "The glue and paper scraper came in, but the paper is on back order. We're stuck with our new friend, Luscious here. At least for a couple of weeks." Carolyn eyes drifted over, "She really is atrocious. Do you think we should try to re-glue the paper that was up there, so we don't have to look at her?"

Denny jerked away from his stare-down with the wall, "Glue the old paper back up? That's crazy. She's not that bad. We'll just turn the light off in here. We hardly use this room anyway, so it's not a big deal."

Carolyn supposed he was right, but still, there was something about the woman on the wall.

—m—

Denny and Carolyn Elliot resumed their lives after that. Denny returned to teaching young people who couldn't care less about the magnificent history he loved, and Carolyn went back to doing her job while her boss, Ed Barlow, took credit for it. Hamsters on a monotonous wheel, they continued their pitiful existence.

The buxom woman on the wall, now nicknamed "Luscious" stayed there. With the midterms under way, Denny was too busy to remodel, and Carolyn was snowed under helping her company prepare for a merger. The wallpaper came in, but was stacked in the corner of the room. They always meant to finish the project, but somehow never got around to it.

Denny, working his way through a fresh batch of term papers, would find himself heading to the kitchen every hour or so to refill his water or to grab a snack from the refrigerator. As he would pass by the dining room on his way to sustenance, he found himself staring at the woman on the wall.

He hadn't noticed it before, but her eyes were a misty blue reminding him of the ocean. He started thinking of the beauty of the salt water and the many ships buried beneath it. There were stadiums full of undiscovered history in those choppy blue waters. Gold doubloons, historical artifacts, clues to history's long unanswered questions. How exciting it would be to have his name on discoveries that could change the world. To be lauded by his peers. To be an explorer of ancient artifacts. Denny felt a push in him that he couldn't keep down. The woman on the wall seemed to be shouting at him now.

ENJOY LIFE

BE THE PERSON YOU WERE MEANT TO BE

Was he doing that? Was he meant to be a college teacher, unfulfilled, whose favorite time of year was his yearly vacation to historical tourist attractions? He dropped the apple he had been carrying and ran back into his study. By the time

Carolyn returned from shopping, he was gone. Denny's hastily written note on the dining room table read:

Have booked a flight to Florida. Getting in on an expedition down there to salvage a wreck.

There was a blank space on the paper and then he added one last line.

I am being the person I should have been.

And with that he was gone, leaving Carolyn to clean up the mess. She had to call the college to tell them her husband needed to take a leave of absence. When they asked the reason, she was tempted to say temporary insanity, but instead she told them it was a family crisis. They said they understood and gave him leave without pay, seeing as they were left trying to cover his classes for the rest of the semester.

Having a new mortgage to pay, Carolyn did all she could not to dip into their savings, or what was left of it after buying the house. She worked long hours and began to resent the executives who depended on her to look good in front of their bosses. About a month after Denny left, Carolyn came home to find him lying on the floor of the dining room, drunk and raising a glass to the buxom woman on the wall.

"Denny?" She said dropping her shopping bag full of frozen dinners for one. "Where have you been? Why didn't you call?"

His skin was brown and his nose slightly sunburned. Even though he looked healthier and much more like the boy she had married years ago, he seemed sad. He barely turned when she entered the room.

"To Luscious," he said quietly as if he were attending the wake of the woman on the wall. He raised his glass and gulped down the contents. Carolyn sat on the floor next to him trying to pull his gaze from the wall.

"Denny! Look at me. You've been gone for a month. You took off for God knows where, and now you show up drunk? What's going on with you? Did you know you're this close to losing your job?"

Denny's eyebrows rose at that news. "I still have a job? Really?"

"Only because I told them you were having a family crisis." Denny, who was mid-swallow, spewed out whiskey all over the carpet.

"A family crisis? That's rich."

"What would you call it then?"

He ran his fingers through his stringy hair. "I'm an ass. A fool. An idiot. Chasing after buried treasure that doesn't exist."

Then he began to cry.

"It was all a con. There was no buried treasure. They took me out on a boat I paid triple to rent and then... no treasure. I was lucky they didn't leave me out there. That's their business you know. Get the people's money, and take 'em for a ride."

Carolyn sat down on the floor next to him."There wasn't any treasure. You were conned?"

"I'm so sorry," he said reaching out for Carolyn and then burying his head in her lap. "I'm such an idiot."

"What would ever make you do such a stupid thing?" Denny stopped his sobbing for a moment and then looked briefly at the wall. The woman's eyes today were a cold gray, the life gone out of them. He couldn't understand what he had seen. Below her cold eyes, her lips seemed to be in more of a smile than he remembered, as if she was about to burst out laughing.

Life after that changed in the Elliot household. Denny ignored the weekly letters from the college and chose to spend his days sleeping in front of the woman on the wall. He pushed the table and chairs against the windows and dragged a sleeping bag and pillow onto the floor.

Most days Carolyn would find him sleeping off another bottle, snoring in the front room as she hurried off to work. Her boss Mr. Barlow had asked her to complete a presentation for him that required many extra hours of work. He was going to be speaking in front of the board of directors and was wanting her to interview forty store managers to get feedback on how the customers were dealing with a price increase that came with the merger. Carolyn had been on the phone almost nonstop, besides doing all of the other tasks she was assigned to. She had been forced to bring other work home and complete it during the evening hours.

Carolyn made a simple dinner of pork chops and rice and sat at the table in the kitchen trying to eat. Denny was in his normal spot on the floor in the dining room, but she could hear him stirring.

"Are you hungry?" She asked. Out of habit she had prepared two pork chops, although Denny wasn't much for regular meals these days.

"I don't know. I'm a little queasy. Maybe a small plate."

Carolyn prepared his meal and placed his plate on the table. Denny did not make any movements in the next room to join her, so she picked up both plates and joined him in the dining room.

"Thanks," Denny said, taking his plate. "I'm a little rocky right now."

Carolyn sat next to him on the old sleeping bag, her eyes searching the mural her husband now chose to spend his days in front of. There was nothing special about this painting. It would never be considered good enough to be called "art". Why was Denny so hypnotized by it? It was nothing more than a poorly drawn greeting card. Be the person you were meant to be? Was this broken-down, depressed drunk on the floor next to her the person Denny was meant to be?

"You've been working a lot lately," Denny said, his voice gruff.

"Yeah, well somebody's got to earn enough to keep us afloat," Carolyn sniped.

"Did you take on extra hours? Because if you did, I'm really sorry..."

"I'm helping Ed. He has a big presentation."

"Ed? The one who never works? The one who lets you do all the work, then claims he was the one who put it together?"

Carolyn avoided his gaze looking down at her freshly manicured nails instead.

"Oh, God. He's got you doing his job," Denny said.

Carolyn picked up her fork and began eating.

"You're better than this, Carolyn. That joker is using you and you know it."

Carolyn threw her fork at the wall. "I had to. Don't you get it? He offered me a bonus if I'd run with this project."

"Is your name on it? Tell me your name is somewhere on it."

"What does it matter? He said he would pay me a bonus. Once I get that money, we can stay in this house for at least six more months. Long enough for you to pull yourself out of that bottle. For you to get your job back at the college."

It was then that Denny realized he hadn't told Carolyn about the letter he received last week ending his position with them. He had meant to tell her, but it never seemed the right time.

"So he is telling the board of directors he did this thing? You can't let him do that. You need to stand up for yourself. You have twice the skills that guy has. Ed Barlow is nothing but a manipulator. He knew you were desperate and..."

"Shut up!" Carolyn shouted. "At least I'm doing something with my life." She grabbed her plate and threw it in the kitchen sink with a crash. Denny went back to the comfort of his sleeping bag. The guilt he felt was unfathomable. His wife had sold her soul, her talent, her brilliance because he couldn't get his ass out from in front of the picture. The woman leered at him now, her breast seeming to be even further out of the red velvet dress. She was really beautiful when you stared at her long enough. He fell asleep thinking of her. He would never paint that wall, never.

Carolyn finished the project at 2 AM, started printing out the agenda, but ran short of paper. She had another ream downstairs and ran to get it in her stocking feet. Her husband's soft snore could be heard from the dining room entrance. The woman in the mural was bathed with light from the hall. After staring at a white computer screen for the last two hours, her colors seemed to be so vibrant, so alive. Carolyn couldn't remember the woman's head being turned toward the hallway.

Be the person you were meant to be. The sentiment went through her head over and over again. Who was she meant to be? She should be doing the job Ed Barlow is doing. Not doing it for him. Be the person you were meant to be. Ed stood in her way. She was sure he was hired over her because he was part of the boys' club. If they knew she was the force behind Ed, maybe she could be the first woman on the board of directors.

BE THE PERSON YOU WERE MEANT TO BE.

ED IS IN THE WAY.

BE THE PERSON YOU WERE MEANT TO BE.

ED IS IN THE WAY.

BE THE PERSON YOU WERE MEANT TO BE.

YOU KNOW WHAT TO DO.

ED IS IN THE WAY.

REMOVE HIM.

Carolyn shook herself awake. What had she been doing? Getting a ream of paper. She pulled away from the doorway, but it didn't matter. She still heard it. Who was the person she was meant to be? She was meant to have Ed Barlow's job. She was the victim of sexism, discrimination, the glass ceiling. She and Ed started out in the same jobs, but he was promoted. He told the higher ups they made such a great team, so they promoted him and made her his assistant. The truth was, they made such a great team because she had done all the work. It was her intelligence that had made their work so good. His gift, it turned out, was taking the credit for it. There was a rolling queasiness in her stomach that was emanating from her anger. Ed Barlow had stolen from her. He had stolen the salary increase she would have had. He had stolen the career she should have had.

"Ed Barlow... Ed Barlow... I hate you. You should die. You should die. You should..."

"Carolyn?" Denny had risen from the floor and was now standing behind his wife. Her eyes had glassed over and her gaze was frozen on the wall.

"Ed Barlow... Ed Barlow," she repeated.

Denny shook her shoulders. "Carolyn. What's the matter with you?"

Her gaze finally broke and she expelled a tired sigh, shaking her head. How had Denny gotten off the floor, she questioned. "I'm sorry. Were you saying something?"

"No, you were. You were talking about killing Ed Barlow."

Carolyn scowled. "What? Are you kidding me? That's crazy."

"Crazy or not, it was coming out of your mouth."

Carolyn yawned. "I'm beat, but at least I finally finished and ready for tomorrow. I'm going to bed." Her eyes met Denny's. "Coming upstairs?"

Denny, his back turned from the wall, put an arm around his wife. "Sure."

The next morning Denny woke alone, in what had become an unfamiliar place, his own bed. Carolyn had already left for the day. Today, for the first time in a long time he felt like shaving. He would take a shower and make a good breakfast, better yet, he would go out for breakfast. He felt like getting out of the house. As he came down the stairs, thirty minutes later, he noticed a bowl of half eaten cereal on the floor. He hadn't eaten cereal last night, so Carolyn must have sat there on the sleeping bag to eat her breakfast. That was unusual, as she usually ate breakfast at the table, reading the news on her Ipad.

Denny thought back to the night before. She had been staring at the wall, repeating the same phrase. After spending so much time in front of the wall, he had felt an unnatural force pulling him, constantly pulling him. First, it filled him full of ambition and then when he failed, it drug him back. Then, he felt powerless, almost as if it fed off of his energy. Spending the entire night away from it, had given him strength. Still, he could feel the pull again. A mesmerizing, comfortable pull. An hour in front of the mural wouldn't hurt him, it wasn't like anyone was expecting him anywhere. He shut his eyes, it was happening again. Denny turned his back on the room focusing instead on the massive fireplace in the den. His gun collection, yes, his love of history. Something wasn't right. One of the guns was missing.

—⁓—

"Carolyn, you're here," Ed Barlow said as he leaned against her tiny office door. "You've been so quiet in here this morning I was getting worried. Are we ready for the meeting this afternoon?"

Carolyn turned from her computer screen, her eyes shining. "Yes. I'm ready." Her voice was monotone and lifeless.

"Well, good, because I've been talking up our presentation." He came in shutting the door and pulled a chair up to her desk. "So why don't you give me the rundown of the presentation this morning, so we're on the same page this after noon."

Carolyn stared now, directly into Ed Barlow's eyes. She didn't speak. She was taking in his request to prepare him for his own presentation. To take her work and take credit for it. The anger inside her was rising from her stomach to her rapidly beating heart. She needed to be the person she was meant to be, a voice said inside her head. Be the person you were meant to be.

Carolyn grinned at Ed Barlow and reached into her desk drawer, her hand now caressing the cold steel of the gun. She was about to be the person she was meant to be. Barlow watched her, expecting her to pull out a chart or a report for him to study. He was surprised when there was a slight click coming from the drawer.

The door of the office slammed open, nearly hitting Barlow.

"Carolyn!" Denny shouted. "You need to stop, Carolyn. Stop right now. You are already the person you were meant to be. Stop what you're doing."

Carolyn's eyes jerked to Denny. What was he saying? His voice was hollow to her. She had to finish. This wasn't right.

"Let go of it," Denny whispered in her ear as he grabbed her hand. "You can't do this. This isn't you. It's her. It's Luscious."

"Excuse me sir, but this is a private meeting," Barlow said.

"This is my wife." Ed snarled, and if you know what's good for you, you'd better leave this office right now."

"I will not." Barlow's face was growing red.

"Yes, you will. Besides that, you're going to need some time to work on your presentation today, because I'm taking my wife home."

Carolyn pushed air out as if expelling the force inside her. What was she clutching inside the drawer? She started to curl her fingers.

"Don't squeeze it!" Denny shouted. Carolyn's hand froze as she realized she was holding a gun. A loaded, cocked gun that was ready to fire.

"Get the hell out, Barlow," Denny shouted. Barlow ran out the door, no doubt to get security. Carolyn pulled her hand out of the drawer, and then set the gun on the desk.

"What happened?" She asked, her head still fuzzy.

"You almost killed Ed Barlow."

"I did?" She stumbled with her words in disbelief.

"It's that painting. It's the woman on the wall." Denny uncocked the gun and hid it in Carol's purse.

At this point, Carolyn would have probably disagreed with him, but she did not. She had come close to killing a person she hated today. It was like someone or something had fueled her frustration. She knew Denny was right.

After that, a for sale sign went up in the yard of 2445 Gossamer Street, and it wasn't long before people started driving by. The property was snapped up immediately because of the reduced price. Carolyn and Denny moved to another city where Denny was happily teaching in a junior college and Carolyn was doing remarkably well climbing the corporate ladder in a new company. Before they left the Gossamer Street house, they covered the woman on the wall with the wallpaper that had been stacked in the corner.

Unfortunately, the new owners didn't care for the color of the paper.

They planned to rip it down as soon as possible.

—ᴍ— ROLL THE BONES —ᴍ—

David Welling

TWO WRONGS DO NOT make a right, so the saying goes. Our wrong was a killer. More accurately, Pete's wrong—he was the person behind the wheel. The rest of us were simply along for the ride.

In retrospect, we all shared in the stupidity that night, since any one of us could have said "No." None of us spoke up. We were all too drunk. Instead, we let Pete take charge, as usual. This is why I am now tied to a chair in a suburban-style dining room, along with my three buddies. Pete, well, what's left of him, is sitting across from me, also tied to his chair. Most of his face is missing. A bullet at close range will do that.

There's blood everywhere—mostly on Pete, but also on the table, the chair, and the goddamned board game in front of me. But not all of the blood is from Pete. Stevie's brains are in the mix. His corpse is tied to the chair on my left. Jeremy is on my right, still alive, still breathing, but with a pallor so white, he might as well be dead.

Then there's the woman towering over us with the gun. She's in the wrong as well, but she doesn't see it that way. She feels she's setting things right. Maybe she is. No mystery there.

"Roll the dice."

Who am I to argue with her? She's got the gun.

With my one free hand, my right is tied behind the chair, I reach for the dice and give them a roll. A seven and a five, enough to get me to the library. It's there on the game board, along with eight other rooms.

I know the game well, having played it many times as a child, a mystery game where the players think like detectives and guess the murderer, the weapon, and where the crime was committed.

There is no mystery here either, since we know who died. We all know the identity of the killer, the place, and how it was committed, even with the additional cards added to the mix. With only Jeremy and me left to play, we try to extend the inevitable by not going for the win.

There are ten suspect cards, the six originally packaged with the game, and four new cards crudely made by hand, one representing each of us. It is a surreal feeling, looking at a game card with my name handwritten in ink accompanying a glued photograph of me. The image is printed from my Facebook page. Not a great picture, but then, I was the one who uploaded the shot. An extra weapon card depicts a car, a 2013 Camaro, just like Pete's.

Then there's the addition to the game board, drawn with a black marker along the right edge, two lines depicting a length of highway. Even without a label, I know which road it is supposed to be and what it means.

"Move," she orders, and gestures with the gun. I shift the token to the library, look at my cards, then at Jeremy.

"I suspect..." Knowing the real culprit, I pick a random suspect and weapon, all the while expecting to feel the force of a bullet. Instead, she turns to Jeremy, who shows me a matching card. I live for another turn.

Shelley is a vision of cold detachment. Her hair is disheveled, as if it has not been brushed in days. Properly styled, the shoulder length auburn hair would beautifully frame an equally luscious face. Striking eyes, a radiant blue. Soft skin. My guess is she's in her mid-thirties. Under other circumstances, she would be drop-dead gorgeous, the source of a million sexual fantasies. She's let herself go, dark circles under her eyes, no makeup, and little attention given to her clothes. Of course, who does she have to dress up for now?

It's a drastic change from the last time I saw her, screaming obscenities in the courtroom as Pete walked out a free man. Involuntary manslaughter, coupled with a DWI, can be a hard rap to beat, but Pete's daddy is rich and has connections. All Pete lost was his precious Camaro, not even suffering a broken bone. But Shelley—she lost her husband and seven-year-old boy in a second as the two cars collided.

The rest of us, we got banged up a bit, some scratches but nothing serious, the worst being Stevie's fractured arm. Yet we still had the rest of our lives before us, while Shelley's had come to an end. How do you repay a debt like that? I doubt that Pete even considered the thought, instead being too concerned about losing his car.

Retribution comes in all forms, and Shelley had it in for all of us, not just the driver. If justice could not be found in the courts, then she would exact it in her own way. So she chose to use her son's favorite board game.

I'm still not sure how she managed to kidnap us all. There seems to be a black hole in my memory over the last day, but when I came to, it was time to play.

It makes sense that I am here with Jeremy. We've known each other since kindergarten, inseparable best friends and all that. We did everything together. It came as no surprise that we ended up at the same college. By comparison, Stevie and Pete were the newcomers, having bonded with us as part of the freshman experience. Pete may have asserted himself as the alpha male, needing that charge to the ego, but it was always just Jeremy and me. The other two were tagalongs.

As a foursome, we landed ourselves into this situation. Once we woke, all tied up to our chairs, Shelley set the dice down on the table, and told us to begin. The gun never left her hand. Stevie was the first to check out from the board game, not fully recognizing how perilous his situation was. He probably thought the gun was a fake. That would explain his attitude when it was his turn. With a stupid grin on his face, he turned to Shelley and said all the wrong words.

"I suspect a dumb bitch who isn't getting enough."

Bad answer. A second later, she pulled the trigger. Stevie's brains and fragments of bone splattered across Pete.

Screaming followed, a lot of it. Pete screamed the most.

And then there were three to play the game. We did so with a terrified but somber resolve. Each in turn, we rolled the dice, moved our tokens to a select room on the board, and made our worst guesses. By then, we all knew why we were there, knew the correct answer—and how it would end if we guessed correctly. With deliberate intent, we moved to every room on the board, anywhere but the hand-drawn highway. Weapons were selected, but never the car. Naturally, we selected the suspects that came with the game, not the new additions. Most likely, she expected one of us to betray the other for a metaphorical 'get out of jail' card. No one fessed up, and so the game continued, round after round, and time stretched to the point of anguish.

However, the inevitable outcome was one of us cracking. Pete broke, with a newfound voice reminiscent of the dog that sees a squirrel and won't stop barking. "Oh, sweet Jesus, help me!" he shouted at the top of his lungs... and continued a non-coherent babble that barely allowed time for him to take a breath. The screaming came to an end only when she aimed and pulled the trigger. I guess she figured it was the only way to shut him up.

Then there were two.

I have no idea how much time has passed since Pete ate the bullet. There's no clock in the room, and the seconds have stretched into hours. The only indicator is the window; through the curtains, I can tell that it's nighttime, the same as when I first woke.

"Roll the dice," Shelley demands. Jeremy does so, pulling up snake eyes, a pair of ones. He gets nowhere on the board. My turn.

The dice take me to a neighboring room, the dining room. I look from the small illustration on the board to the room around me. It is decorated in a mediocre fashion, suggesting a lack of taste in Shelley's style. The furniture is well-worn solid wood with floral design pillow chairs. Mass-produced prints of landscapes and feel-good quotations adorn the walls. Shelves hold an array of paperbacks and knick-knacks. Nothing matches. On a corner cabinet sits a vase with flowers, all withered from lack of water. While I'm no fashion designer, it is clear that she desperately needs an interior makeover.

However, there are pictures. Lots of framed photos all around the room, shots of a father and son, along with some group shots with the mom. I'm not sure if it is meant as a shrine or a reminder. Probably both.

I make my guess with the cards, picking the woman with the red name. All the suspects have names based on colors or food condiments. I also pick the wrench, knowing that the tool is incorrect. It has no wheels.

My eyes meet with Jeremy, and something seems to snap. He takes in a deep breath, as if accepting the finality of his position, and gives me a weak smile.

She shifts the gun in his direction. "Roll."

He shakes his head. "No." He speaks so softly, it is nearly inaudible.

"I said roll the dice."

"What's the point?" This time, he speaks louder, the despair evident in his voice. "You've already killed two of us. I don't think you'll let either of us go. I can't handle this anymore, so you might as well get it over with."

He locks eyes with her, and in that moment, I realize how strong he really is. I don't have the balls to say that.

She stares at him, considering his words, and for a brief moment, there seems to be a reprieve from this horror. Something inside her moves, a note of compassion. The moment is fleeting. She takes a step towards him.

"Fair enough."

Jeremy's head explodes in a spray of red, coinciding with the recoil from her gun. My friend, who I have known since childhood is gone in an instant. All the potential he had before him, all his futures, successes, loves and hates—everything he might have been, now is reduced to a lifeless mass of flesh.

And in that moment, I know Shelley. I feel her anguish. As alien as the thoughts are, I understand why she stands there with a gun in hand. In that moment, we are one, and I am willing to help her pull the trigger a final time.

A heavy breathing assaults my ears, and I recognize it as my own, sharp intakes of air, and my body convulses with each breath. In the distance, there is another sound, sirens, but I am unsure whether it is my imagination at play.

This time, there is no need for prompting. I roll the bones, knowing this is the end game, and move my token to the one place on the board left to go. It comes to rest on the highway.

Our eyes connect and I see the darkness within, a lonely void where once there was life.

Companionship.

Joy.

She watches as I lay my cards down in the pool of red that covers the game board.

"I accuse myself and Pete, Stevie and Jeremy with a Chevy Camaro on Highway Six. God forgive us all."

As the words come forth, so do tears, and I taste the salty flavor as they reach my mouth. My eyes remain trained on Shelley, on her emotionless face, not the instrument in her hand. The sirens grow louder.

Her voice is soft, but with a razor's edge. "You feel it now, don't you."

All I can do is nod.

"What it's like to be left with nothing. Except memories. So many memories. It hurts."

The siren reverberates against the walls, as if it's right outside the door.

She raises her hand, wiping it against the wetness of her nose. "Billy loved this game. We played it every day."

Somehow, I manage to find the strength to ask. "You let him win, didn't you?"

"Every time."

Voices call from the other side of the door. The sound of pounding, fists against wood. Someone wants in.

Shelley sniffs, wipes her nose again. "You're different. You have a heart. I hear it beating."

Of course she can. If feels as if it is about to burst. With another step forward, she raises the gun, aiming it right at my chest. I know what she wants to even the score. My beating heart for the silence of her lost family. A simple pull of the trigger will set things right.

The pounding on the door grows louder. Then something slams against it, breaking it down.

Tears are streaming from her eyes now. "You know what grief is, don't you?" The gun never wavers, remaining fixed on the spot at the center of my ribs. "How it feels? How it eats you up from the inside?"

Footsteps echo across the front room, leading to us. Then comes a man's voice, authoritative and with a single purpose. "Lady, drop the gun."

She ignores the intruder. "Consumes you until there's nothing left."

I manage to whisper a single word. "Yes." This is more than an answer. It is acceptance.

Shelley looks at me, and for the first time, she smiles. The expression conveys a wealth of feelings, mixed with loss, bitterness, and consent to the inevitable. The way a mother might look at a wayward son. Then, aware of what will follow, she spins around, the gun moving from my chest to a target she knows it will never reach. Time distorts and she moves way too slow.

Shots are fired. She falls to the ground, another mixing of blood to that already spilt.

And now there is one.

In the aftermath, once I have been untied and led from the room; after the ambulance and the questioning; after I offered my best answers; after the funerals for three friends, there comes the deadening lull. I realize that I have been left with a mystery, one that has nothing to do with the board game. It has nothing to do with Shelley's kidnapping of four teenage boys, or why she murdered three of them. I know those answers. I felt what drove her to it.

It has to do with redemption. Shelley played her last hand as she always had before, knowing that the game was over. The die had been cast.

But for me, I will be rolling the bones for years to come.

~~ BLOOD-RED GERANIUMS ~~

Patricia Flaherty Pagan

EVERY SUMMER AT Maplewood Farms, bees dip and rise as if spreading the story of Chico's disappearance. Irises wave in the wind. Lavender plants huddle and guard the secret.

"I don't know any Chico," Julian says.

In my mind, I still hear his words and wonder.

~~

July heat rises off of the metal hide of the coffee truck as if it were a silver armadillo. I squeeze into line behind the pickers, trying not to look at their brown, taut muscles as they buy bottles of juice or gnaw on sticks of beef jerky. Flushed, I stare instead at the caked black earth crawling up their work boots. My young adult brain can't decide whether it is racist to think about how the Haitian guys wear muscles better than the Irish and Italian-American boys in my neighborhood. The owners have bussed pickers down from the fields in New Hampshire. Usually Maplewood reflects enough of the idyllic fantasy of farm life to keep Ann Taylor-wearing housewives flooding to the painstakingly-decorated farm stand and garden center, but, during a harvest, many hands must work the land. Fresh crops demand care, sweat, and blood.

From an old boom box adorned with a Kiss 108 FM sticker someone has left on the picnic table, Boyz II Men sing "End Of The Road." Behind me in line, the head picker, Chico, holds his work radio like a microphone. He steals the chorus and weaves it into his own love song sung in a mix of Spanish and Haitian Creole. I turn to watch him and Chico bends in an exaggerated bow.

Danny cuts into line in front of me, nonchalantly holding *The Boston Herald* under one arm. "Mau-reen, string bean," he says into my left ear. "Where you been all morning, sunshine?" I blush. His ginger hair and goofy smile complement his freckles. The farm stand cashiers often say he's cute, 'in a Larry Bird kind of way.'

"Hi, boy, it's hot!" I stammer. Why didn't I take the job at Express, folding skinny jeans? Why had I let my love of fresh air drive me into a mix of budding plants and teasing men?

The produce guys stroll over to Danny with a pizza and a six-pack of Coke. I am thwarted yet rescued by their argument about the best pitcher The Sox ever had. As the young men walk off together, I buy a turkey sandwich. Nausea churns in my stomach. I surrender my lunch to the wasps.

An hour later, I am calf-deep in Liberty Hosta in the greenhouse when Danny returns. I have nowhere to hide. My fingers peel off browning leaf after browning leaf and drop them into a yellow, plastic bucket. Relentless heat pounds down from the solar panels. As he balances a tray of blood-red geraniums about to sprout in one hand, Danny stops and blocks my path with his broad shoulders.

"So what do college girls do at night? Calculus? Read poetry?" His lips turn up at the corners.

I watch a fat drop of sweat slide down his neck and resist the urge to wipe it away for him.

"My mom is into Emily Dickinson. Dragged me all the way out to her museum," he continues with a laugh. "I pretended to hate it, but it was OK."

Green leaves and bright blooms form a cocoon around us. I inch closer. His musky smell draws me to him.

"You wetback shithead!"

We turn towards the shout and hear a grunt followed by a muffled cracking sound. We can't see much, but I imagine work boots connecting with bone.

"We'll get the berries in without you half-wits! Take your Español and your Creole gibberish back to your own countries!" A man yells.

Gasping, I turn to Danny, but he has already set the budding perennials down and dashed through the open door. I sprint after him.

Rob, the landscaping manager, clasps a silver flask in his hands. Over and over his right foot cracks into Chico's swollen head. Writhing, Chico tries to ball himself up to protect against the blows.

"Stop!" Danny says.

Rob stumbles, drops his flask and lurches in Danny's direction. Despite being twice Danny's age and wobbling from drinking too much Wild Turkey, Rob manages to land a right-handed punch on Danny's upper arm.

"Back off, man. Pancho Villa is getting what he deserves," Rob slurs.

Instinctively, I hurry to Chico and cradle his head into my sweat-stained t-shirt. Trickles of blood roll down the Maplewood Farms crest.

"Are you all right? Chico? *Chico!*" A shrill voice rises, and I realize that it's my own.

Cashiers abandon their registers and rush out of the stand as Rob shouts about hell and "bastard Mexican immigrants." Two cashiers debate whether to call the owners or the ambulance, and two of them argue about whether Chico comes from Colombia, El Salvador, or Mexico. Suddenly, Rob rushes Danny. Danny coldcocks him.

"Call…" I begin to yell to the group of cashiers but falter. "Call 9-1-1!" Chico's head drifts slowly to one side and his eyes glaze over.

A dusty Ford F-150 screeches in, and Julian, the farm manager, jumps out. He gestures at Sully, the six-foot-two supervisor of the field workers, and at two muscular Hispanic men whom I do not recognize. Julian pulls me out of the way, and then he and the other two men descend on Chico and the fighters. I can't tell whether they are there to help, or harm, the fallen Chico.

Marcy, the head cashier, walks out of the stand, takes my arm and leads me, along with all the other young women, into the sweet-smelling fruit market."Ambulance?" I ask.

Moving her hand as if erasing a blackboard she says merely, "Wait."

We hear Julian's truck pull away. Looking out a window, I see that the plants in the yard are the only remaining witnesses. The twenty-foot journey to the pay-phone looks like a million mile trek. I shiver. Mud and blood clump under my fingernails. Determined not to be the fragile college girl, I bite my lip and will myself not to cry.

"You'll be working in the shed. Wash and glove up and go box berries," Marcy says to me softly, her order an attempt at soothing.

"I'm on perennials."

"Not anymore," she says as the light drains from her eyes. "Don't worry. Julian will deal with this. He'll call the doctor, and the cops if he has to. He always… handles things."   For the next two days, my gloved hands scoop plump straw-berries into green boxes. 'Runts' and 'squishers' I set aside for my breaks. Each time, I stare at the payphone across the yard, I wonder when Danny will return, and forget to eat the strawberries I've saved for myself.On the third day, a navy blue Crown Victoria rolls into the lot. A trim man with buzz-cut black hair walks past the open doors of the work shed, through the farm stand, and towards the office. Paramount Pictures' casting department could not have brought in a better police detective. Alone in my berry-stained refuge, I hold my breath. Curiosity pulls me into the fruit market to learn what's going on. A cashier named Jennifer stage whispers to another cashier, Ali, who stage whispers to the next one, the word "homicide." When the detective walks out again, I run to the tiny bathroom and throw up.

At the end of the shift, Julian calls all the employees out into the yard. His considerable bulk blocks my view of the payphone. He breaks into his wide, family-farmer smile he usually reserves for tanned housewives shopping for fresh corn.

"Good work today, team," Julian says, wiping his sweaty brow with a blue bandanna. "So, you may have some questions, or hear other people asking questions, about the incident that happened with Rob a couple of days ago. We all need to be on the same page. To work here together," he pauses. "Since he was insubordinate and drunk on the job, I fired Rob. And Danny has a lot going on in his family, so he had to resign."

"Huhs?" and "Whys?" rise from the gathered workers.

"He said to tell Maureen and Jennifer goodbye," Julian continues. Someone in the crowd snickers and my cheeks burn. "Sad those two men had to go. Listen, if we are going to keep *working together*, we need to be clear on what happened."

No one responds to the implied threat. Julian rubs his chin and waits.

"Chico?" Janjak asks. The group of pickers around him murmurs in concern.

"I don't know any Chico," Julian says.

—⟶— FLOWERS FOR LEWIS —⟶—

Mary Jo Martin

CAMDEN, SOUTH CAROLINA WAS a quintessential Southern town, with a flower-filled Main Street lined with little shops and eateries that catered to locals and any tourists who happened by. It brought songs like "Summertime" to mind. On the surface, it was a place where the living was easy. Not too big, not too small. It was close enough to the capital of Columbia for bigger city offerings. Like most places, Camden also had a darker side. There were skeleton-filled closets and unspoken current-day scandals that people never talked about except in polite whispers. But it wasn't the kind of place where you'd expect a murder.

Lilly Langford was born and raised there, to a socially prominent, but financially stressed family who'd lived in the area for centuries. One of her ancestors was a Revolutionary War Patriot, a woman, who at the tender age of thirteen, performed valuable services for the American cause by spying on the British troops in the area. Lilly's Aunt Martha wrote a historical novel about this little patriot. The book held a special place in the Langford living room, providing a constant reminder of the family's place in society and its proud heritage.

Lilly's family was filled with strong women, but she wasn't one of them. Although she was a smart, beautiful child, she did not inherit the confidence that so many of her ancestors had possessed. Nor did she have any athletic skills. Growing up, Steven, a more aggressive playmate, would constantly tell her, "Get out of the way, Lilly, you're no good at this game." She'd immediately run home crying.

Lilly went through the customary rites of passage that prominent families put their daughters through, like coming out parties, cotillions, and debutante balls, charming the local boys along her journey. Suddenly, those boys realized that the awkward Lilly of their childhoods had become a stunning young woman. No matter how hard they tried, she wasn't attracted to any of them. Lilly knew far too much about their histories and their families. The town was filled with stories of whose mother was sleeping with so-and-so's father, and which business people were diverting money from their partners. She vowed she'd never marry any of them.

One day, while working in her Aunt Martha's antique shop, a Yankee named Lewis Bacon came into the store. Lewis was "from away" (the polite Southern term for a Yankee). He was the oldest son of a Boston Brahmin family, traditional upper class, and a Mayflower descendent. He'd come to South Carolina to continue his Revolutionary War studies at the University of South Carolina. His focus was the Southern campaigns, and this gave him a good reason to escape from his stuffy, overbearing parents, who tried to rule every aspect of his life. While making small talk about the shop's offerings, Lewis held up a pair of vases and asked, "Are these really antiques or do you buy them from China?"

Lilly wasn't sure if he was joking or not, but liked his audacity, saying with a twinkle in her eye, "We have a lot of history in the South, you know." Picking up on his Boston accent, she followed with, "Y'all up North aren't the only ones with old things."

Lewis was attracted to Lilly's elegant body, long blond hair, and playful light green eyes, as well as her ease at repartee and charming South Carolinian accent. He was over six feet tall, with dark, wavy hair and cobalt blue eyes that sparkled when he was teasing. He was easy to look at. Their brief exchange proved to Lilly he could be funny and charming, instantly improving Camden's ambiance. Most importantly, he was not a local boy.

They saw each other frequently when Lewis came to Camden to study the archives at the battle field. It started with visits to the shop, which soon led to dinners. After a whirlwind courtship, they married, and that was when Lilly discovered Lewis's charm was an extremely thin veneer.

Although he occasionally drank wine on their dates, it turned out he was an alcoholic, an ugly drunk. He took out his repressed anger against his overly controlling family on Lilly, beating her cowering body until his blows left bluish purple marks. But he was a cunning abuser. Lewis only hit her on the upper arms, legs, and torso where there wouldn't be any obvious visible marks. Beyond the physical attacks, he demeaned her constantly, frequently telling her, "Stop being such a spineless bitch. I want a woman who'll stand up to me." Lilly wore long-sleeved clothing and slacks. She was too intimidated to stand up for herself or leave him. As a woman in such a situation, you had only two options: fight back or suffer in silence. Lilly chose silence. And that silence was deafening.

Lewis's family didn't attend the wedding. They fumed over the fact their oldest son, and heir to their family fortune, would dare to marry some nobody who was not a proper Bostonian girl. They nursed their anger, telling each other how Southerners were lazy and sloppy, even in their speech. They withdrew even further into their exclusive Boston enclave.

Not soon thereafter, Lilly became pregnant. She hoped that would make things better with Lewis. It might give him a chance to be a better man, and stop drinking, at least for the sake of the child. Her family and friends were thrilled, especially when she announced at her baby shower she was having twin girls. She hoped and prayed Lewis's parents would come around, now that they'd have grandchildren. But they never even sent a card when the twins were born. Lilly and the girls were not part of their world.

Gracie and Callie started life strong and kept getting stronger as they grew. When other kids in school pushed one of them around, the other pushed back harder, even giving one bully a bloody nose. They both had short fuses, just like their Daddy.

As little girls, their favorite thing to do was dissecting bugs and frogs. Gracie and Callie decided science and medicine would be good careers, and they had the brainpower and determination to do it, as they were always at the head of their class and consistently winning science fairs.

Growing up, they watched as their father slapped their mother for even minor things like forgetting to get the mail. He constantly dominated her verbally, telling her what a weakling she was. And yet there was their mother's deafening silence. It was frustratingly hard work to keep their tempers in check.

By the time the twins entered high school, Lewis was a Professor at the University of South Carolina in nearby Columbia. He taught Early American History and had swarms of young co-eds swooning over him, his Boston accent, and his provocative ideas about sexual revolution.

One student in particular, Ellen Shaw, had a nearly pathological crush on him. She shadowed Dr. Bacon around campus every chance she got. Although he didn't always appreciate the "chance encounters," he secretly enjoyed the attention, and was oddly attracted to this peculiar young woman. She was nothing like Lilly. Ellen was strong-willed, with dark brown curly hair and mysterious eyes that followed him at every opportunity.

What Ellen didn't realize was she had an admirer of her own, who always sat in the back row of her lecture halls, and shadowed her on campus, but was too shy and afraid to approach her. Unfortunately, Ellen was too busy stalking Lewis to realize he existed.

One day, Gracie and Callie came home from a party to find their mother beaten again. Callie stamped her feet and shouted, "Mama, some day he's going to really hurt you, and then what? Will you still stay with him? Why don't you leave him?"

Lilly tried to soothe them, saying "I'll be fine. They're only bruises, and they'll heal."

Gracie cried, "You won't be fine! Why can't you pack up and go stay with Mee Maw? I'm calling the police."

"Put that phone down. What would the neighbors think if the police were parked outside our house? I could never abandon your father. And your grandmother couldn't handle us living with her. Most importantly, it would be a family disgrace. Do you want us to be like one of those families people around town gossip about?"

Callie screeched, "So, it's better to wait until he kills you?"

Lilly was horrified her daughter would suggest such a thing. "You know he'd never do that." And yet, as the words exited her lips, Lilly felt fear and doubt creep into her heart.

The twins stomped off to their room, furious at their mother for her weakness, but even angrier at their abusive father. This had to stop. Callie told Gracie, "There must be a way we can help Mama. We're smart, let's think of something."

The following week, Lewis came home from the university smelling of Scotch, as usual, and staggered through the door. He wasn't fully drunk until he dove into his stash at home. He sat alone in the den in his usual place with the lights low and the television off. Without any warning, he became violently ill, with vomiting, diarrhea, and a frighteningly irregular heartbeat.

Although the girls detested how he treated their mother, their father had never laid a hand on them, and a father's love was a father's love. Along with Lilly, they took shifts sitting by his bedside, checking his pulse and trying to get him to drink some water. He ignored them, and refused to go to the hospital, slurring, "Just cheap booze. Lemme alone, I'll sleep it off." Within hours, he got weaker, his pulse fainter, and he lost consciousness. Before an ambulance arrived, he died.

Lilly was wracked with grief at losing her husband, and the girls deeply mourned their father's passing, but they were all secretly relieved the abuse would finally stop.

Callie told her mother, "I thanked God the nightmare is over. Is that bad?"

Lily embraced her daughter but didn't say a word.

Gracie, the practical one, asked, "We won't have to give up our home, will we?"

Lilly reassured them that they'd be fine, "Your father had a good job, and a trust fund from his family. There was life insurance on top of that, so we'll never have to worry about money."

Since Lewis had never shown any obvious signs of poor health, an autopsy was performed. The Kershaw County Coroner, Dr. Agnew, reported that Lewis had died of natural causes, a massive heart attack.

Within a few months following his death, Lilly, Gracie, and Callie were beginning to rebuild their lives, and the once silent home was now filled with joy and laughter. Then Lewis's father unexpectedly arrived in Camden, and the fleeting freedom Lilly had gained slipped from her grasp. Dr. Thomas Bacon was a well-known cardiac surgeon, a large, imposing, red-faced man with a temper, who was used to getting his way.

The day he appeared unannounced at the house, he talked to Lilly, Gracie, and Callie. The girls told him about the alcoholism and abuse.

He sputtered in disbelief, "My son could not possibly have done those things."

Lilly lowered her gaze but finally plucked up her courage and told him much more directly than most gracious Southern women would, "I am sorry to tell you this, Dr. Bacon, but Lewis was a son of a bitch. I can assure you that he was an alcoholic, and he repeatedly beat me after he'd had too much to drink." Then she crossed her arms, raised her head, met his gaze directly, and finished by saying, "And that's all I have to say about that."

Callie chimed in, "We loved our Daddy, and we're sorry he died. But we hated what he did to our mother."

Gracie, ever the peace maker, tried to soothe his anger and pride, saying, "We miss our Daddy very much and can't stand that he died so soon. It must be hard to lose your son. What can we do to help y'all get over your grief?"

Dr. Bacon suspected that Lewis's death may not have been quite as natural as these women thought. And, he wondered if they had any part in it. He stormed out of the house, saying, "That boy played lacrosse all through school and had a heart like a horse. We'll see if this death was from natural causes."

His next step was a personal visit to Dr. Agnew. "May I see the full autopsy report on Lewis Bacon?"

Agnew informed him, "I'll need to get permission from Mrs. Bacon for that."

Lilly, of course, agreed, so the coroner shared it with him. That's when he learned at least part of what Lilly had told him was true. Even after losing so much fluid, Lewis's blood alcohol level was still above the upper limit of legal intoxication. But Dr. Bacon knew that alcohol alone would be unlikely to kill someone, even at those high levels, so he was still suspicious.

By the next day he was convinced there had to be foul play involved in his son's death. He tapped into his network in Boston and had them arrange for an order to exhume the body. Normally, this wouldn't be executed so quickly, if at all, but Lewis's family had tremendous influence that extended even into the depths of South Carolina.

The Camden Police Department opened an investigation. Two seasoned detectives, Walker and Sherman, were assigned to the case. They began to look into Lewis's life. After questioning Lilly, Gracie, and Callie, they learned Lilly had been repeatedly beaten after Lewis's drunken interludes.

Walker told Sherman, "I'd bet money these women had something to do with his death. Between the wife beatings, and all that money they stood to gain from his wealthy family, they sure had a good motive. If we can just break them, we can make a good case."

Lilly, Gracie, and Callie all admitted to being home at the time Lewis became ill, so none of them had an alibi.

The detectives worked with the Columbia police, and in interviewing some of Lewis's students, uncovered the story of Ellen Shaw, the co-ed stalker.

They spoke to Nina, one of Ellen's girlfriends, who told them, "Ellen might have been crazy, but she had a thing for Dr. Bacon and was sure she could talk him into leaving his wife and live with her here."

Sherman told Walker, "If Ellen figured she'd rather have Lewis dead than lose him, she's a person of interest. Now we have four possible suspects."

They interviewed Ellen, and, although she was what Southerners call bat-shit crazy, she had an air-tight alibi. She was in the emergency room having her stomach pumped from an overdose of sleeping pills on the day Lewis fell ill. The hospital records and the ER staff confirmed her story. "I thought if Lewis heard about it, he would rush to my side and we could finally be together. I couldn't have killed him. I loved him desperately, and living without him would have been miserable. In despair, I tried to kill myself over his lack of attention."

Walker told Sherman, "Damn, now all we have is the family."

Sherman agreed, saying, "Lilly's close to her daughters, and turning them against each other won't be easy. So, we should split them up."

Dr. Agnew reviewed his autopsy results, but didn't find anything he might have overlooked. He pulled a blood sample from the exhumed corpse and ran more tests. That's when a trace amount of something other than alcohol showed up. Camden's limited lab facilities were not able to determine exactly what it was and the amount was barely detectable. He reached out to Dr. Springfield, the Richland County Coroner in Columbia, where they had more sophisticated lab equipment.

Springfield told Agnew about their findings, saying "We discovered the same thing you did. We're not sure what it is either, but I suspect it might be a cardiac glycoside, since it looks similar to what we've seen in digoxin overdoses." He went on to explain, "Cardiac glycosides include a range of compounds from life-saving digoxin to highly poisonous substances. They're found in a variety of common garden plants, including Lilly of the Valley and Oleander. They interfere with the heart's electrolyte pump and cause a buildup of sodium and calcium ions in the heart muscles."

Agnew asked, "If the sodium and calcium concentrations get too high, wouldn't they trigger a fatal heart attack?"

Springfield said, "Absolutely."

South Carolina overflowed with beautiful, lush plants and flowers. But some of those plants, especially the Oleander, were poisonous. Every part of the Oleander was toxic, from the flowers and leaves to the roots. Southerners knew this, so they were careful to keep their kids and pets away from it. People didn't even burn the wood, since the glycoside was not destroyed by heat, and could be inhaled in the smoke, causing the same lethal effects as swallowing parts of the plant or extracts made from the leaves. But, cases of Oleander poisoning in the US were rare; even coroners like Agnew and Springfield would not consider it first as a cause of an unexplained death.

When news of these findings reached the detectives, pieces of the puzzle began to fall into place. Gracie and Callie knew from their own experiments how easy it would be to extract compounds from plant leaves. They could mash the leaves, mix them with alcohol, let them sit for a while, then filter out the mashed up leaves to get a clean extract. Access to alcohol was a snap in their house; Lewis always kept a bottle of Everclear on hand in case he felt he needed more of a jolt than his favorite Scotch gave him. The twins not only had a motive, but the intellectual and physical means to concoct a special cocktail for their father.

The problem the detectives had was trying to prove it. They started by attempting to break Lilly. But Lilly, out from under the spell of a domineering husband, embraced the mental toughness of her female forebears. After all those years of being controlled by Lewis, and encouraged by her daughters, she vowed she would never allow that to happen again. Lilly drew herself to her full height, looked Walker and Sherman directly in the eye, and told them, "I did not kill my husband."

The interviews with Gracie and Callie did not go any better. Walker and Sherman interrogated them together. Walker threatened them, "You know that if you don't cooperate, we can take you away from your mother."

In separate interviews, Sherman told Callie, "Your sister rolled on you, and the best you can do is tell the truth and help us solve this case." He went on to say, "We'll do all in our power to get each of you a light sentence. We know there are extenuating circumstances." Walker did the same with Gracie.

It was all in vain. Gracie and Callie knew how to deal with bullies, and they were their Daddy's daughters. They kept reminding themselves of their young teenaged Revolutionary War Patriot and how she spied on the Redcoats. This was nothing compared to that. Plus, they knew they were innocent. Gracie and Callie swore that although they were overjoyed that their mother was not being abused any more, they loved their father and had nothing to do with his death.

The detectives got a warrant to search their home. By then, Dr. Springfield's lab results convinced them Lewis died of Oleander poisoning. Walker tore apart the kitchen and the garage, thoroughly searched the girls' room, and swabbed down every surface he thought could have been in contact with alcohol or plant parts. Sherman confiscated all of Lewis's bottles of alcohol. They seized the family computers to see if they'd done any searches on cardiac glycosides, but found them clean as a whistle. Even the computer forensics experts in Columbia didn't find anything. The only fingerprints they found on the bottles were Lewis's. They had the samples from their swabbing analyzed in Columbia, but found nothing that matched that trace compound. They searched the yard for signs of Oleander cuttings, but the yard man had just finished pruning all the bushes, so everything was cut. As far as evidence was concerned, Walker and Sherman were stumped. They had no case.

Meanwhile, Dr. Bacon was becoming more and more frustrated with every passing day. He brought in a private detective from Boston, Frank McGillicuddy, who'd been Superintendent of the Bureau of Investigative Services before he retired.

McGilicuddy visited with Walker and Sherman and offered to help them with the investigation. Although resentful of interference by this from away outsider, they finally agreed to work with him. He started by reinterviewing Lilly, Gracie, and Callie. He had no more success than the Camden detectives and was convinced they were all innocent. He talked to Dr. Agnew and Dr. Springfield.

Although no one could prove it, like Walker and Sherman, he knew in his heart someone had killed Lewis by Oleander poisoning. The question was who and how.

As a last-ditch effort, he went back to Columbia and talked to Lewis' students. Carol, one of Ellen's friends whom the Camden detectives had not interviewed, confirmed Ellen's attraction to Lewis. More importantly, she revealed Ellen had an admirer and a stalker of her own. Joshua King was a shy boy with a bad temper who was a graduate student in chemistry.

Carol told him, "Joshua had fallen hard for Ellen, but she had a single-minded mission, and it was Professor Bacon. Joshua did confide in me, though. That's how he learned Ellen didn't even know he was alive. He became convinced Professor Bacon was leading her on. And that made him furious."

McGillicuddy, working with the Columbia police, brought Joshua in for an interview. He was no match for the Boston investigator. After being interviewed for hours, Joshua finally broke. The wave of confession that followed was almost too good to be true. "I started following Dr. Bacon, and discovered that he went to a bar near campus in the late afternoon. I trailed him there one day and confronted him, demanding that he give up on Ellen. I swear, I never planned to kill him. I just wanted him to stop encouraging her."

Joshua said that Lewis told him, "Don't be ridiculous, boy, I don't care anything about her. But you could do me a favor and tell her to stop following me around. It's getting old."

Joshua, incensed over this response, shouted, "Dr. Bacon, I better never see you with her again. You leave her alone." He stormed out of the bar with clenched fists and began to hatch a plot to take Lewis out of the picture for good.

The following day, he followed Lewis again, hanging in the shadows of the bar, waiting for Lewis to go to the men's room. Once he did, Joshua made his move.

That was the night that Lewis became so horribly ill. McGillicuddy confirmed that the bartender had seen Joshua in the bar arguing with Lewis, and then saw him again the following day. The next step was to search his apartment. The Columbia police got a warrant, and worked with McGillicuddy, Walker, and Sherman to swab surfaces and confiscate his laptop. They found all the evidence they needed to charge him. There were traces of oleander extract all over his kitchen, along with a bottle of alcohol, and a mortar and pestle for grinding the leaves. On top of that, his laptop contained a full history of searches for cardiac glycosides. Joshua might have been a good student, but he was not bright enough to clean up after himself.

The case was tried in Columbia, in South Carolina's Fifth Judicial Circuit. The Circuit Solicitor, who fills the role of a District Attorney, was delighted with this air-tight case. The jury took only two hours to reach their verdict. Joshua was convicted of first-degree murder, and sentenced to thirty years in prison. Ellen, delusional as ever, began to visit him in prison. She realized she had someone who loved her enough to kill, a passion like no other.

After the hubbub of the trial, Camden began to return to normal, with its citizens going back to their favorite steeplechase races and polo matches instead of constantly sitting around gossiping. Parties, cotillions, and debutante balls returned with their usual regularity. With the tension gone, ladies began lunching more on Main Street, and eventually the talk about Lewis Bacon's death and the Langford family subsided. The university found a new professor of American History, a rumpled fifty something, not-so-debonair fellow with a wife and three children. He didn't charm the co-eds as Lewis had. Those girls even learned some history.

Lewis's father was finally vindicated, and was pleased McGillicuddy and the Camden and Columbia police got the killer. McGillicuddy got a huge bonus, and Dr. Bacon made generous contributions to both police departments' fund raising efforts.

Before returning to Boston, he began to have second thoughts about how he had treated Lilly, Gracie, and Callie. Although he was opposed to the marriage, they had all been kind to him. And the girls were his grandchildren. He visited them to offer his apologies and asked, "Can you possibly forgive me for being so rude to you?" Raised to be gracious women, they accepted, and hoped that a new family relationship might develop. But then, Southern women are always hopeful, aren't they?

THE MIDAS TOUCH

Joyce Kopp

CRISTINA RAISED HER champagne glass to make a toast to her girls, her gold mine. "To each of you. For your hard work, your awards and your million-dollar contracts, I congratulate you." Bowing her head, she searched for words. "Unfortunately, three girls are gone." After a brief pause, sensing an emotional outbreak, she rallied, "Next year, I promise, shall be better, thanks to *you* all still here. Now, let's celebrate our accomplishments. Bon appétit!"

They had sweated their way through the usual morning at the gym, followed by a rare gift of Thai massages at the Crescent Spa on Spring Street. Now they chatted over a light lunch at Manhattan's latest foodie spot, Luigi's, a place to be seen and to become known.

Cristina, director and newly inherited owner of the modeling and photo agency, Valdez Studios, watched over her models as they dined on shrimp scampi served on beds of mixed greens bathed with a lemony aioli sauce while sipping cucumber water with slices of lime. She was a proud sentinel, guarding not only their waistlines but also their reputations. Well-dressed in Versace and Karan, poised, and flashing dazzling smiles, her girls attracted countless admirers. For the males daring enough to approach the table, Cristina quickly shooed away with a backward swat of her hand in the air and a glaring gaze.

Having finished her lunch and after checking her Rolex, she sharply clapped her hands together to stop the chatter, "Time to go, girls." They grumbled but obeyed, grabbing their cashmere scarves from their Valdez monogrammed totes in order to protect their necks from the December cold. Snapping her fingers over her head, Cristina demanded both the check and her white Mercedes. The four ogled colleagues scrambled into the car as Cristina tipped the valet and haughtily took over the wheel.

As she maneuvered through the traffic back to the studio, she dictated the afternoon's agenda, "We're doing a piece for *Life and Leisure*, first as tourists in Acapulco. No need to change now. Later we'll do the beach scenes, so don't forget to bronze up for a beautiful glow."

Meanwhile back at the brownstone in Brooklyn Heights near the East River, Mark, a forty-something, six-foot-two, lanky-legged and broad-shouldered former male-model turn artist and photographer, was waiting for them. Lights, cameras, mural, props and soundtracks stood ready for staging and ambiance. With a push of the button to start the music and action, the girls strolled and chatted as tourists, gesturing and laughing, twisting and turning, posing on cue, as Mark captured it all on film. When recorded sounds of thunder threatened and lights dimmed, they turned and glanced east and west, questioning and pouting.

Displeased with the action, Cristina shifted to the edge of her chair. Perched there, rolling her eyes, she interrupted the shoot, "Cut!"

"Mark, stop the CD!"

"Consuelo, sway those hips when you walk!"

"Nika, fold your hat brim back just a smidge, so we can appreciate those beautiful dark black eyes!"

"Angie, listen to the soundtrack! It's going to rain and ruin your day. I know you can pout better than that!"

"Mark, perhaps a little more purplish overcast. See what you can do with the lights!"

Cristina settled back into her director's chair, furiously tapping her nails on its arms. "Okay, girls, let's start this scene over. Mark, dear, before we begin, please get me another Perrier."

As Mark dropped everything and obediently fetched her water, the girls were whispering amongst themselves and moaning.

Christina barked, "No moaning! Just get it right this time!"An hour into it, Cristina signaled the end of the shoot, clapping her hands over her head. "Swimsuits! Back in five! Don't forget to bronze up!"

The models hurriedly removed their high heels and dashed to the back dressing rooms. They emerged wearing the latest fashions in beachwear and feigning their best smiles.

Another forty-five minutes into the late afternoon, the girls massaged each other's necks and backs, relishing any seconds off-camera. All but Cristina were ready to call it a day. She demanded more close-ups. The girls stifled their moans.

Mark, obsequious, wove his broad shoulders and camera between their bodies, deftly changing colored lenses to mimic golden sunrises, cloudy afternoons, and violet sunsets, now stooping and shooting up, then standing on tiptoe. Winking, grinning at the ladies, elbowing, pinching them, blowing kisses and whistling, he caught their candid expressions as they reacted.

Suddenly, quite unexpectedly, Consuelo slumped onto the Brazilian hardwood floor with a resounding thud, her voluptuous body perfectly still, with the heel broken on her right stiletto, half-crushed under her swollen foot. The other three models, Nina, Miko, and Angelina, screamed and jumped back, horrorstruck.

"Mark, dial 911!" Cristina directed. She raced over to the fallen Venezuelan beauty, dropped to her knees and ripped open Consuelo's beach cover-up, watching her chest, hoping it would rise and fall. She listened for her breath. "Mark, she's not breathing!"

"911 says to check for a heartbeat, check for air obstruction...tilt her head back.

"No, ma'am, not breathing. How many compressions? Fifteen and two quick breaths? Okay, come quickly. Valdez Studios on Oak, #34. Yes, ma'am," Mark screamed to the 911 operator.

Feeling helpless, Cristina sprang up, tearing at her short black hair, her eyes piercing through the dark silence, and shrieked, "Sabotage! It must be! Who else but Tom Markell! He's stolen Moon-Sun from me, and now he's killed *three* of my beauties!" She raged around the room. She clenched her fists in the air. "First Raquel, then Fiona, and now it appears, maybe Consuelo! He will surely pay for this!"

Mark countered, "Calm down. Maybe it's a seafood allergy from what she ate at lunch." He sprinted over and began to give Consuelo mouth-to-mouth, counting the seconds while rapidly pressing on her chest.

Cristina paced, pausing to command, "Girls, take a break. We'll finish the shoot tomorrow...or the next day, we'll see...after all this is cleared up." She shooed them away. Huddled close, sobbing, leaning on each other, the girls stumbled to the back dressing room.

Cristina pointed to the spotlights, "Mark, shut them off. We're done for the day."

"But...Consuelo...." As he continued the chest compressions, sirens blared, becoming louder and closer.

Cristina snapped her fingers and pointed first toward the lights, "Off," and then the door. Reluctantly, Mark interrupted his CPR. The vivid blues and oranges of the Acapulco mural backdrop dimmed to a stark grey. Collapsing into her rose-colored director's chair, Cristina pulled her ivory scarf tighter around her neck and her knees up to her chest, rocking back and forth as she stared at the lifeless silhouette of Consuelo.

The sirens were replaced by flashing lights pulsating upward from Oak Street through the jalousies and bouncing through the darkened room. On the way toward the door, Mark stopped to massage Cristina's neck, leaning over to kiss her pale cheek. "Don't fret, love. Help's here."

Boots were heard stomping up the brownstone's steps followed by a knock at the door and loud male voices. Quickly Mark ushered the emergency team in. Spying the girl on the floor, they rushed with their defibrillator to revive her, but her pupils were already fully dilated, her lips blue-tinged, and her face swollen.

Cristina paced again and wrung her hands, muttering, "Markell must pay. I shall demand a full investigation. Never will I have to worry about him again!" She kept pacing, her thoughts whirling–*A decade of bribing and stealing her models after she had trained and coached them, taught them the art of flirting with the camera. Now it appears they might all be in peril of flirting with death. What has he done to them? Courted them, now poisoned them?* "Of course," she cried aloud as she wore a path across the staging floor, "I must first interrogate the girls. Maybe I should hire bodyguards, better yet, a private investigator."

Her mumbling was interrupted by the chief medic, a muscular, stocky fellow with caring eyes. "Ma'am, pardon, name's Eric. I can see you are quite distraught. It appears the young lady has died of asphyxiation. Is she your daughter? A relation?" To each question, Cristina shook her head no. "Do you know what killed her?"

Her eyes shot darts, her voice blared, "Not what, who! I know exactly who's done this!"

Eric whipped out his cell. "Ma'am, I'm calling the police. They'll be here shortly. Save your breath until they arrive."

This time, she nodded affirmatively, then swallowed hard and dabbed her eyes. Eric bent over the body, and with his fingers, he brushed the girl's tawny curls off her flawless face and closed her eyelids over her baby blues. He then traced his finger over the arc of her nose, over her swollen lips, and down the curve of her neck to her bosom, where he made the sign of the cross. He instructed his assistants to bring in a body bag. A tear slid from the corner of his eye. "A real beauty!"

Next, he addressed both Cristina and Mark, informing them that he needed to write his report and they would have to answer some questions. He suggested she get some water, and she willingly disappeared. He eyed Mark, "You have a different theory?"

His only reply was "No, sir."

Meanwhile, an officer appeared. "Captain Charles," he coughed. Eric raised a questioning eyebrow. "Flu season. Short on staff tonight. Otherwise, I'd be holed up in my warm office." He only took one glance at the body, photographed and taped around it, then waved to the medics to dispose of it. He then proceeded to interview those present.

"Captain Charles," he reintroduced himself, politely removing his hat when Cristina reappeared, as Mark ran to her side, offering to carry the bottles of Perrier. She gestured for them to be seated at the Italianate-tiled table with coral padded chairs in the adjoining room.

Throughout the questioning Cristina indignantly tapped her long pink-man-icured nails on the tabletop as she spoke. She ranted and reiterated her belief that Tom Markell, her competition, was behind all of this, declaring he was jealous of her girls, who had been featured on the covers and inside the magazines *Divine Beauty* and *Best Travel* within the last year. Each had since received offers for skin product endorsements and free travel photo ops, which she herself was entitled to a portion of their remuneration, according to their contracts.

"Tom has been slowly stealing my girls from me the last ten years," she complained, "offering them more money and more perks: all-paid non-working vacations, monthly spa treatments, jewels included in the wardrobe. It's killing my budget and my bottom line. He's costing me millions! Plus, I spend intermi-nable hours training them. And now, if that's not enough, if he can't persuade my girls to join his team, he's somehow killing them! Three in four months! I sweat and fret over them. He has to be stopped! I demand justice and retribution!"

"And Consuelo, the one you found…" she glanced up at Eric as she wiped the tears streaming from her eyes, "had just been awarded Model of the Year at the annual convention in Costa Rica. She was honored not only for her professional modeling, but also for the charity work she has done for the impoverished in her native Venezuela, especially helping to create safe exercise facilities for the youth after school. She was worth her weight in gold!"

"She was a real beauty," Eric repeated, shaking his head.

"I see," Captain Charles replied stone-faced, still taking notes diligently. He turned toward Mark, "Anything to add?"

"I know nothing about the business competition. The girls are great to work with. Love them all. Otherwise, I'm only the photographer and assistant, dutifully employed, sir."

"I see," the Captain scribbled again.

Eric inquired, "Before we leave, may we speak with the other girls, Ms. Valdez?"

"Oh! I don't know! They seemed so upset! I don't know if they'll want to talk now."

"Would you mind asking?"

"No, no, of course not…" Cristina cleared her throat. "I'll check on them."

Moments later, she emerged embracing her slender dark-haired Angelina, almost a foot taller than herself. "My daughter," she smiled, "the others appear to be too exhausted. I didn't want to wake them. They need their beauty rest, you know."

Eric and Captain Charles simultaneously stood up as Eric offered her an empty chair, "Please, just a few words."

"Of course, I understand. We want you to get to the bottom of this. Three girls de...gone within the last four months. We're all frightened."

Soft-spoken Angelina nodded and readily answered their questions. Upon request, without hesitation, she neatly printed the other girls' contact numbers. Her long black bangs cascaded over her wet green eyes as she pushed the tear-streaked paper across the table.

Captain Charles pocketed it and tipped his hat on their way out the door. "I'll be in touch."

A bitter wintry wind blasted their faces as they descended to the street. Pulling his collar up around his neck, Eric remarked, "The ladies had such a golden glow, especially for this time of year, did you notice?"

"No, I hadn't. I'll add that to my notes. Thanks. I think I'll have my best detective check out those beauty products Ms. Valdez mentioned, as well as this Tom fellow." They shook hands and departed.

Several weeks elapsed before Sergeant Timothy O'Connor reported back to Captain Charles. First, he said he had interviewed the three girls present on the day of Consuelo's death. He had ruled out any motives for poisoning, that none of the girls appeared to be jealous of Consuelo winning the top modeling award and that they all appeared to be very amiable, almost like sisters. He had also interviewed two others on the list, a Lola and an Adriana who had been traveling in Greece at the time of the incident. In addition, he had paid a visit to Tom Markell, a graying middle-aged man who he thought was quite business-like, with an impressive MBA from Harvard, and rather likeable. Mr. Markell had sincerely expressed his condolences and had sent flowers to Ms. Valdez. "If I may say, Captain," the Sergeant added, "personally, I thought he was on the up and up, displayed no malice and was much more congenial than Ms. Valdez."

The Captain smiled. "Thank you for this report, Sergeant. It moves the investigation right along. Have you received an official report from the coroner?"

"Only that asphyxiation was confirmed, with no apparent reasons noted. At this time, Captain Charles, I would like your permission to follow these young beauties for several weeks."

"Yes, of course, just be aware they are on edge, frightened that they may be next on the killer's list."

"I'm aware, sir. No worries. They won't know. They don't call me the 'Silent Sleuth' for nothing."

Three weeks later, he reported that a Vincenzo Carmini had been dating two of the girls, Lola and Adriana. He was suspicious of this "Romeo."

The following week, another frantic 911 call came in just after midnight. This time the call came from Angelina at Gold's Gym. Swift arrival by EMT at 12:26 a.m. Lola was pronounced dead by 12:30 a.m. Sergeant O'Connor was already there when Captain Charles entered and pulled him aside, "Do you think our lover boy, Mr. Carmini, was responsible?"

"No, I don't think so," O'Connor replied. "I was told the girls had been throwing medicine balls and practicing yoga during a photo shoot, when Lola collapsed."

Now the girls were sitting on the floor, once again sobbing, sweat running down their faces and dripping down their necks, glistening on their skin, their hair clinging to their faces. Golden rivulets formed puddles in several spots on the floor…except for near Lola.

O'Connor steered the Captain toward the front door, out of earshot. "I followed Lola tonight. She had visited the tanning salon on Pin Oak before she came here. Another half hour to overheat her body."

He then strode over to a promotional display by the front door and picked up a jar of cream called "Midas Touch," which was advertised as producing a beautiful healthy glow. He opened the lid and swiped the cream, placing it on the back of his hand. "It has a golden glow, doesn't it? Look closely. It contains microparticles of gold. Gold when heated to a certain temperature, say in a tanning booth, in a hot gym, under a photographer's lights, will melt and close the pores. The skin can't breathe, plus the strenuous physical exertion, and the person dies of asphyxiation. I believe Lola and the others were all innocent victims of the 'Midas Touch.'"

Captain Charles grasped the jar in his hand, searched the fine print and found no warnings on the label, only a signature name of *csantiago*. He had a daughter too. His brows furrowed. What if she would buy this product unknowingly?

He stormed over to the huddled group and his voice boomed out, "Do you girls use this product?"

Sheepishly, they replied "yes" in unison and squirmed uncomfortably in answer to his booming voice.

"Who is *csantiago*?" his face puffed angrily as he read the label. They furtively glanced sideways at each other, taking a code of silence, and lowered their eyes to the floor. Captain Charles lowered his voice, "This could be your killer. And you're wasting my time. But I'll wait."

The girls looked puzzled and remained silent. Only the clock on the wall ticked, interminable minutes and seconds, ominously passing.

A threatening statuesque figure, the Captain eyed them like a hawk and didn't budge. Finally, Angelina stammered, "My… my mother, Cristina…her late mother's name, Carmen Santiago. She and her husband Carlos were the prior owners of Valdez Studios. Carmen was also a chemist and developed the beauty product. Cristina thought it gave us a golden glow and requires that we use it at every shoot. She's been trying to market it, and the gym was kind enough to let her promote it."

Sergeant O'Connor quietly explained the dire situation to the ladies while Captain Charles turned his gaze toward Cristina, who had turned pale and was inching toward a side emergency exit.

"Stop!" Captain Charles barked. A few strides, and he placed Cristina's hands behind her back, while firmly speaking into her ear, "You are currently under arrest on suspicion of involuntary manslaughter."

Speechless, she grudgingly tramped beside him toward the front door.

"You have the right to remain silent…"

Meanwhile, Mark had stood motionless against the wall in the back of the gym, silent, taking it all in, and even now, not rushing forward to be by Cristina's side, offering his undying support. Instead, he secretly smiled inwardly, savoring his thoughts of becoming the new owner or co-owner of Valdez Studios and treating the girls as his treasures.

THE MANSION

Andrea Barbosa

I FIRST NOTICED HER on a summer afternoon, as I strolled leisurely along the shaded avenue. Admiring the monumental houses on the south side of the city, which stand in magnificent view and boast historical markers, she was a contrast against the others. Although all the mansions were still inhabited, she stood alone and abandoned. The grass on the front yard hadn't been mowed for at least a couple of months, and climbing vines grew up the wall to the second floor. All the windows were shut with curtains now stained by time.

I approached the front door where the marker was. According to the history engraved in the metal plaque, she was built by a successful lawyer of the region, and later sold to a rich businessman who purchased it as a gift for his bride. The historical significance was due to the beautiful architecture, in colonial revival style and with an engineered peculiarity for the time period she was built, around 1925.

She was rather wide looking from the front. I counted twenty windows both up and downstairs, but her width was only one room deep. Walking around her and puzzled by this oddity, the feeling of breaking inside was taking shape in my mind. Would she be empty or furnished? What was her secret?

I walked back to the front door and tried it. Dust and cob webs fell over me. It was locked, of course, so I peeked through the beautiful glass framed door hoping to have a glance of the interior. What I saw seemed to be the main entrance, where an ornate staircase undulating like a snake towards the second floor stood. I could see no further. Darkness and an eerie quietness surrounded me. Defeated, there was nothing left to do but forget about the magnificent mansion and resume my relaxing walk.

After I became aware of her, though, the mansion would permeate my mind with a steady curiosity, and I found myself instinctively making detours to drive by her more than I needed to. I wondered what mysteries would be hidden inside, feeling compelled to look at her, as if she was observing me, as if she was staring back at me whenever I was within her surroundings. There was a weird feeling behind all the magnetism drawing me to her, and I recognized she was challenging me, but I didn't know if I was prepared for it.

A few months later, as I continued to be drawn into driving by my abandoned mansion, I spotted an elderly man working in the front yard. It was the first time I saw someone around the property. She must have been bought, I thought. Not able to contain my curiosity and feeling somewhat possessive and jealous, I parked in the driveway hoping to talk with the presumed keeper. I didn't want anyone finding out her secrets before me. After all, she had been summoning me now for months. I got out of the car and walked casually up to him. He ignored me with the indifference of a medical examiner towards his murdered patient, moaning words in a not-at-all welcoming way.

"It's not for sale," he whispered.

I attempted to be as friendly as I could,

"Oh… I thought it was… it is such a beautiful place! Do you live here?" He stopped trimming the bushes and looked suspiciously at me, eyeing me from head to toe for the first time since I approached him.

"What do you want?" I couldn't tell exactly what I wanted or why I had stopped by, but I had to question him to find out more about her.

"I was wondering… is this mansion abandoned? I mean… someone must have just bought it, right?" The man didn't seem eager to talk.

"No. Nobody has lived here for more than sixty years if memory serves me right." My determination did not retreat, since this was the first time I saw a live person in the mansion's immediacy. "So, why isn't it for sale? Why is it abandoned?" He appeared tired; surely a man his age taking care of a huge house's landscaping was not an easy task. He sat down on a boulder close by.

"Look. The house is empty. It's not for sale, nobody lives here. I take care of the grounds every once in a while although I'm too old now and can hardly mow the yard. Why do you want to know about it, anyway?"

It was going to be hard getting any information about the destiny or past of the mansion from this man. Why was he so unfriendly and cautious about it? At least what I had feared the most was not so, no one had bought her. But I still hadn't satisfied my inquisitiveness.

"Who owns the house? The historical marker says it was bought by a businessman for his bride; is it still owed by his family?" The old man shook his head.

"I don't know." He got up and resumed his work, without glancing at me any further. The conversation was over.

I gazed at the mansion. I felt her insistent and quizzical stare upon me. There was definitely something uncanny and mystifying about this place. My proximity to her this time gave me an even bigger impression of being observed, and it made me nervous. I was fascinated yet horrified. Something about the mansion disturbed me. I was obsessed about her, and I knew she was defying me. But after this somber encounter with the mansion's groundkeeper and the chilling feelings of being watched, I had to stop this madness. I avoided passing in front of her as much as I could, and deliberately tried to block any paranoid thoughts about this damned fixation.

One evening, while I was out drinking with friends, the mansion came up in our conversation. I don't even remember what prompted it to be a topic of discussion when someone made a bet and I was drawn into it. A month's rent for whoever broke into the mansion alone and explored it that same night, bringing back something as proof of their audacity.

"Come on, Mayer, you love that old house, get yourself over there!" I knew I was out of my mind when I accepted the crazy deal, fueled not only by my friends' words of encouragement when they cheered me by my last name, but by an irrational jealousy from thinking anyone else but me could violate the mansion. Thus, I drove by myself to the inexplicably fascinating house.

As soon as I parked in the long driveway, I felt compelled to give up and forget all about the absurd challenge. Nonetheless, I knew I had accepted the bet not for the rent, but because of my curiosity and pride. For some strange reason, the mansion was a big deal to me, and I had the courage to enter her, or so I thought. The mansion knew me, and I felt like the only one with access to her.

I got out of the car after carefully hiding it behind high bushes and trees, picked up a stone from the driveway and threw it with all my strength into one of the upstairs windows. It broke instantly, but all I heard was the crack of glass crashing on the floor. No alarm. But she heard me. She woke up. I was sure she could sense me and feel my apprehension. She knew I was there. The mansion was a living monster and it was ready to swallow me.

I walked towards the back of the property, trying to find a way to get in, when I noticed a broken window barricaded with what seemed to be a heavy and discolored curtain. Dogs started barking in the distance and the light of a nearby house was turned on. I hid among the trees and didn't make a sound.

Once it was all back to silence, I penetrated through the window as noiselessly as I could, shifting the heavy curtains blocking my way. And suddenly, I was alone with the darkness. It had been so easy to enter her. I turned my flashlight on and my exploration of the first floor started. I found myself in what seemed to be the dining area; a large, decorated room. The walls were covered with several paintings and portraits of beautiful women. Upon a closer examination, though,

I realized it depicted the same attractive woman portrayed in different attire and moods. She was young and pretty. In the center of the room, a huge rectangular table stood with only three chairs, although it could comfortably fit more than fifteen. Two silver candleholders still bore the waxy remains of long ago burned candles. Before leaving the dining room, I glanced back at the woman's portraits. She was simply alluring.

The next room was a library and the shelves were still filled with books thickly covered with dust and webs. I read some of the titles and was surprised to find biographies of famous European Renaissance painters: Bellini, Raphael, Michelangelo and Titian, and complete collections of works by Shakespeare, Flaubert, and de Maupassant, among others. Books in German, French and Italian, different volumes of Bibles, and a shelf filled with business, administration and accounting books completed the archive. In the corner of the room, a desk was cluttered with papers yellowed by the passing time, as if forgotten in a living museum.

Stationery papers and envelopes with the initials SMG adorning them were scattered around. I wondered whose initials these were. As my curiosity grew deeper, I opened different drawers in search of more clues, but there was nothing else to be found except handwritten accounting books, and some old newspaper clips dated from the 1940s. A good proof of my breaking into the house would be one of those dated newspaper clippings, as well as a sheet of SMG's stationery paper. I folded what I needed and enclosed them with care in one of my jean's back pockets before resuming my exploration.

Three more rooms to be inspected downstairs turned out to be the kitchen, a living room and a quite spacious area next to it, which was evidently a ballroom, with a single piece of furniture at one corner: a white grand piano. Looking further into these rooms would not do anything else to satisfy my yearnings for the mansion's secret, so I headed for the entrance chamber and climbed upstairs, as the bedrooms seemed to be a more exciting choice for me to examine and dig into the lives of the mansion's last residents.

A long corridor revealed itself empty and all the doors were closed. A chill ran through me, for I was deep inside her now, and it was too late to give up. She seemed to urge me even more inside of her. I was in a state of panic. I already had proof of my breaking into her. Hadn't I already proven my courage? I should leave, but why was I tempted to stay? She had conquered my senses and I didn't have the willpower to abandon her. I needed to satisfy her lust as well as mine.

Her heart was beating like my own, yet I didn't know where to begin the search and what I was looking for.

With shaky hands, I turned the knob of the first door to my left and, with a shrieking crack, it opened up and I stepped inside. The flashlight exposed a fairly large chamber, and its walls bore heads of animal trophies. Surely the last inhabitant was a skilled hunter, and one who was proud of his captures: heads of bears, deer, bulls, even a lion peppered the walls. I almost tripped, as the floor was also crowded with carefully mounted stuffed animals, no doubt the work of an expert taxidermist. Those were domestic pets, as well: dogs, cats, rabbits, birds and sheep. What a petrifying vision! I left the pet cemetery in disgust, just to step into another mortuary room filled with the same odd and ghostly decoration. Dozens of animals! Two rooms filled with these creatures! What kind of crazy people had lived in such conditions, surrounded by dead pets?

There were another four rooms for me to look into, but the musty, humid smell of dust and animal furs nauseated me. I forced myself to move on, despite my growing suspicion. To my relief, both the third and fourth rooms were empty. The fifth one sported a large bed covered with beautiful laced sheets, and black furniture consisting of two chairs and a desk. There was a gentleman's hat still laying over one of the chairs and when I opened the closet, I found men's and women's clothes hanging, ready to be worn in a long ago past. Somehow, this gave me the impression the couple had left in a hurry, leaving behind all of their belongings.

When I moved on to the last room, I hoped there would be no more surprises and that all I felt about the mansion was just a quick bout of paranoia. The door was locked. What could be the secret; was there one? Maybe it was just another empty room, maybe another one full of macabre stuffed animals. I could take a guess and leave without bothering with it any longer. But it was the last room, and I knew I wanted to open it.

I forced the weight of my body against the door, and after a few strokes, it broke open. The first thing the glow of my flashlight fell upon was a terrifying vision. A large four post bed placed in the middle of the room contained the creepy remains of a human being's skeleton resting on it. When I turned the flash light around, I was suddenly face to face with the pretty lady portrayed in the pictures downstairs, who stared at me wide eyed like a wax figure in a horror movie. Before I could even think, I felt a touch on my left shoulder and jumped back, screaming.

The groundkeeper stared angrily at me. I was petrified and could barely move my lips, which were frozen in a shocked and silent scream.

"What is the meaning of this?" I asked once I was able to somewhat compose myself. The aged man glanced at the mummified body of the lady in sorrow and hesitated.

"This is Mrs. Suzanne Mayer-Greenfield, the wife of Mr. Eugene Greenfield, a successful businessman back in the 1940s," he started. This time, his tongue was not tied.

"SMG..." I whispered, realizing the initials of the stationery I got from downstairs were hers. How odd. My last name was Mayer. When I was a child, I recalled an uncle telling the story of a past relative who supposedly traveled overseas with her husband, but no one ever heard from her again. Could it be?

"Why is... she...?" I pointed at the embalmed body, unable to finish my question.

"Mr. Greenfield, he... he had a demented, crippled brother who was kept locked in this room. He was not allowed to interact with anyone, except for Mr. Greenfield himself and a few of the servants." I looked back at the human bones set on the bed.

"Is... is that him?" The groundkeeper nodded.

"He was a skilled taxidermist, Mr. Greenfield's crazy brother. So Mr. Greenfield would often bring him game, any animal he hunted, even farm animals to keep his brother busy," he explained.

"That's why the other rooms are filled with them," I thought aloud.

"Yes. It's all his work. But when Mr. Greenfield brought his young bride to live in the mansion he bought for her, he warned her about his deluded brother." I looked at Suzanne again. Her beautiful countenance, so perfectly portrayed in the paintings, was preserved for eternity.

"She was a very delicate and sensitive lady, and she felt sorry for the unhappy creature. She pleaded with her husband to include him as part of the family so he could, perhaps, live more humanly and develop social skills." I turned around to gaze back at the man telling me the story and interrupted him.

"How do you know all this?"

He paused, then replied, "I've always been an employee of the Greenfields. Do you want to know the rest or not?"

I sensed his impatience and asked him to continue. He began with a sigh.

"Reluctantly, Mr. Greenfield gave in to the wishes of his beloved lady Suzanne, and introduced the beast to the beauty... The thwarted brother, who had never seen such a fine-looking human being before, was bewitched by her kindness, patience and purity. Indeed he became friendlier, and after a while Mr. Greenfield allowed him to dine downstairs with the couple." I couldn't help interrupting him once more.

"The three chairs in the dining room... it makes sense." He sighed again before continuing.

"Despite being insane and deformed, though, he was an artist at heart, a skilled and lost soul with the need to express himself. So he painted portraits of the woman with whom he developed an obsession, for whom he seemed to live.

He dared not touch her, as his brother never allowed them to be alone, but in his mind, I knew a growing desire to possess that treasure was burning. He became jealous of his brother and his manners worsened. Afraid he might become dangerous and hurt his wife, Mr. Greenfield locked him back in his room and forbade everyone to go see him, especially Mrs. Greenfield".

I nodded for him to go on.

"On one occasion, when Mr. Greenfield was out of the country on a business trip, Suzanne heard the cries of the imprisoned beast and opened the door to meet her fatal destiny." His voice lowered to almost a whisper. My heart beat fast, expecting him to deliver the horrible news of Suzanne's demise.

"She tried to console him, that's what everyone assumes, and he was probably very happy with her presence. But when she attempted to leave his room, the hysterical creature feared never seeing her again. He then choked her to death, embalming her precious body as his trophy."

I gasped in disgust. What a terrible fate!

"She was missing for days... the house staff and I searched for her to no avail... until Mr. Greenfield came back from his trip a week later. In despair, having no apparent clues as to the disappearance of his wife, he went up to the creature's room just to find her as you can see her now: cold, petrified, exhibited as a prize for the delusions of his abominable, repulsive brother. In his agony, he locked the room back, leaving the beast for starvation with the mummy of his lost love. Mr. Greenfield left the house as soon as he was sure the crazy murderer had died, and the house has been neglected since. No one knows what happened to him, but his estate covers the expenses. I am just an old and faithful servant and I've been taking care of the house since he abandoned it. But I'm too old now; I can't keep it as good as I used to before."

I looked around again. Suzanne stared at me. I was completely horrified by this macabre spectacle. I wanted to leave and forget this bloody mansion, but somehow, her static eyes beheld a warning expression. How could this be? All of a sudden, through the reflection of my flashlight, I glimpsed the shadow of a butcher's knife about to strike me. It was the groundkeeper! Why was he trying to hurt me? In a quick instinct, I moved swiftly out of his reach as he accidentally tripped and fell upon his own deadly weapon, stabbing himself.

I glanced at Suzanne, stupefied. What was the meaning of all this? She was smiling at me. I thought I was going insane when I heard her melodious voice. She sounded relieved, in peace, as if her soul had just been avenged. Her voice was calm, soft and low. I listened to her in bewilderment while she narrated her version of the story; the truth about her death.

"The gardener was obsessed with me, so when my husband went overseas for business, he saw his opportunity to have me. I fought back fiercely to keep him away from hurting my integrity and devotion to my husband. He didn't take no for an answer and inadvertently strangled me to death, while trying to keep me still." I couldn't believe my ears. A murdered woman, dead for many years, was telling me her version of the crime that killed her.

"Afraid of the consequences of his impulsive actions," she continued, "the murderer decided to blame my death upon my husband's unstable brother and threw my lifeless body inside this room. When the poor creature found my dead body, he tried to reanimate me to no avail. He could only do what he thought was right, and obviously he was held responsible for such unspeakable crime. You are a Mayer. I knew I could call upon you to rescue me." And in the blink of an eye, she was silent again, back to the wax figure she had become.

Somehow I had been chosen to avenge her death and punish her real killer after so many years. I was proud of myself. All this time, the impression of being observed had always been Suzanne calling out to me. I closed the door to the frightening room and quickly left the house and its mystery solved behind me. Had it been a dream?

I never told my friends, who were waiting for me at the bar, anything about what had really happened inside the mansion. Who would believe I had avenged a ghost? They were excited when I pulled the old newspaper clip from my pocket and showed it to them as proof that I had entered the abandoned mansion. I won the bet, of course, but I kept the stationery with Suzanne's initials for myself as a memento of our secret connection. Later that night, I drove in front of the mansion on my way home from the bar and looked up at her. She was smiling at me.

AN EYE FOR AN EYE

Meg Lelvis

"WHAT'VE WE GOT," Lt. Jack Bailey asked an officer at the scene ten miles from town. A twelve-year veteran with the Richmond, Texas police, Bailey was irritated at the interruption of his evening at home. Second time this week.

"A kid. Single car off the road, smashed that tree pretty good," Hector Reyes said.

"Jesus. Kid's been identified?"

"Yeah," another officer answered. "Brace yourself. The Bradford kid— Bart. DOA."

"Well, there's one for the papers," Bailey's voice sardonic.

He knew the untimely death of Bart G. Bradford II would be no shock to the community. Four prior DUIs and no jail time. Public outrage poured out against Bart's light sentences, especially for the vehicular manslaughter of one Trevor O'Neal three years ago when the Bradford kid ran a stop sign and plowed into Susy O'Neal's car. She survived, but two-year-old Trevor died en route to the hospital.

Steady rain fell as a wailing mass of patrol cars, an ambulance, fire truck, and a dozen police officers crowded the scene, turning the ditch and ground to muck. Flashing lights blazed against an inky, sinister sky.

"What else you got," Jack Bailey asked.

"Tonight around ten thirty Bradford's BMW flipped to one side and crashed into that oak," Reyes answered. "Got an anonymous 911 call. First responders were the Richmond volunteer fire dept."

"What about ID?"

"They identified him by his wallet found on what's left of the car seat," Reyes continued. "Three EMTs spent fifteen minutes cutting and pulling Bradford's mutilated body from the wreckage. He was probably traveling at least ninety miles per hour, judging from the impact result."

Call the ME, Lieutenant?" a rookie cop asked Jack Bailey.

"Naw, non-suspicious accidents don't require it. But they'll do toxic screening."

Jack Bailey was not what people would call a friendly, soft spoken guy. A salty, fifty-eight year old cop from the old school, he was tough, hardened, and did not mince words. Tall and solid, his face reflected a brooding, tragic expression. Some people called him a dead ringer for Liam Neeson. Bailey's dark hair fell over half his forehead, and sharp blue eyes seemed to bore through those who dared speak to him. His chiseled profile boasted an aquiline nose and prominent jawline.

He hated useless social niceties and cut to the chase. No 'how ya doin' crap for him. Nor could he tolerate committee meetings and bureaucratic management protocol. Yelling at his cops was enough management for him.

Bailey was friends with only two or three officers, one of whom was Moose LaGuidas, who approached him through the rain.

"Where were you," Bailey growled as he popped a green Tums. Damn acid reflux never let up.

"Where do you think at this time of night!"

"Glad we can bury this pain in the ass case. I'll deny it if asked, but that spoiled prick finally got what he deserved. You didn't hear that, Moose," Bailey said offhandedly.

"Hear what?" They both chuckled.

—⁓—

Moose LaGuidas's stature bore no resemblance to his nickname. A lean man of medium height with dark blond hair and green eyes, he'd been a Houston patrol officer for a couple years until he made sergeant. When his wife insisted the city was a dangerous pit, and they better leave or else, he transferred to Richmond, a small town forty miles west of Houston. People found Moose affable, an all-around nice guy.

Bailey continued to supervise the usual procedures at the scene. After transport of the body to the morgue, he told Moose, "Gotta go notify the parents now. God, I hate this part."

"Why not send Nolan? She does better with these things."

LaGuidas referred to Kathleen Nolan, an officer known for her diplomacy and compassion.

"Naw, gotta do this myself. Old man Bradford would wonder why the top dog he's been trying to bribe for years didn't show."

Barton C. Bradford was the town's wealthiest land developer and its foremost citizen. He was well known in business circles in Houston, as well as Dallas and other Texas cities. He'd gotten his son off four prior DUIs and criminal mischief for the usual reason: He hired the best lawyers and bought off the most crooked judges money could buy.

The rain poured down as Jack Bailey pulled on a yellow rain cape. He walked up the winding brick sidewalk to the Bradford home which proudly displayed a historical registry plaque. Outdoor lights showcased the house against the night like a lighthouse emitting a blinding light.

He rang the doorbell three times before a Latino housekeeper in her bathrobe peeked through the window and inquired who was ringing the doorbell at one o'clock in the morning.

Bailey held out his badge and was ushered into the vast foyer. As the housekeeper disappeared from the room, Bradford and his wife Nancy scurried down the stairs, took one look at Bailey and groaned, "Not again."

Nancy Bradford, a petite blond woman, wore a long ivory silk peignoir set and looked attractive and elegant as her society page photos, even at this late hour. Her husband, as burly as she was small, tied a maroon terry cloth robe around his ample waist and attempted to straighten his shock of white hair.

"Let's go in the den and sit down," Bailey's voice soft. He shrugged his rain cape off and hung it on the high end hat rack.

"What did he do this time?" Bradford asked as he led the way through the foyer.

"What is it? What happened—is Bart okay?" Nancy Bradford grabbed Bailey's arm, her expensive manicured nails leaving dents on his skin.

"Sit down, Nancy," Bailey indicated the white leather sofa. He waited until both parents settled onto the couch and then began slowly. "This is never easy. Bart was driving alone in his car. He swerved off the road and hit a tree outside of town. Happened around ten thirty this evening."

"Oh God, oh no," chorused the Bradfords. "Is he okay?"

Bailey waited and looked grim. "I'm afraid he didn't survive."

"No—what—no," both parents cried simultaneously. "You can't mean, are you saying

Bart's d-dead?" Nancy sobbed, her hand flying to her mouth.

"Oh fuck, oh fuck," moaned Bradford. "He said he was doing fine after this last rehab stint. He was wasted, right?"

"We'll do a tox screening in the morning," Bailey answered cautiously.

"Oh God, my baby, my baby, it can't be," Nancy buried her face in her husband's chest, choking on her sobs.

"I'm sorry. I'll give you a few minutes, and then I'll need one or both of you to come with me for the necessary paperwork," Bailey said. He walked into the foyer and chewed a white Tums. He gazed around at the vaulted ceiling, gilded mirrors, and winding staircase. He'd always felt disdain for the wealthy, but surprisingly, he had a modicum of sympathy for the Bradfords. Rich or not, Bart was still their son. They'd probably be kicking themselves the rest of their lives for being too soft on the kid, for spoiling him and not holding him accountable for his actions.

—⚭—

The next morning across town, Dave O'Neal sat at his kitchen table and opened the front page of the *Fort Bend Herald*. He gasped at the headline. His heart thumped, and his hands shook as he read the article. His wife, Susy, came into the kitchen and headed for the coffee pot.

Dave held the paper toward her. "Look at this." She skimmed the short article.

"My God, Dave, can you believe it?" She poured herself coffee and paced the floor.

She started crying softly, then her sobs became louder.

"No, Hon, I can't believe it, but justice is finally served, justice for Trevor." He rose from his chair and embraced her.

"Yes, finally justice," Susy said through her tears. She poured a shot of Amaretto into their coffee for a celebratory toast. They clinked their cups together.

She took a sip. "Maybe the nightmares of that horrible day will go away now."

After three years, the pain of losing her son was still raw. At least now that monster wouldn't kill any more innocent people.

They gulped down the spiked coffee. Dave said, "I'm calling Jack Bailey. Get more details."

—⚭—

Moose LaGuidas stuck his head into Bailey's perpetually cluttered office. "You got a phone call. Yours just goes to voice mail." He held out his cell to Bailey.

"Hell, the phone's been ringin' all morning. Who is it?"

"Dave O'Neal."

"OK," Bailey said. LaGuidas stepped into the office, closed the door, and handed over the phone.

Three years ago, O'Neal, Bailey, and LaGuidas communicated daily regarding the investigation of young Trevor's death. After Bradford's trial, they remained in touch and eventually became friends.

"Yeah, Dave," Bailey said. "Imagine you're shocked. Right, DOA. Don't know the level yet. Don't have the tox report."

"Yeah, everything in the article is right on. I'm sure more will come out later."

"Actually, I thought of that since the rain didn't affect the road conditions, but I'm sure he was one drunk bastard."

"OK, Dave. Maybe congratulations are in order." Bailey hung up the phone.

LaGuidas got up from the chair, retrieved a file from the floor and said, "How did he take that 'congratulations' comment?"

"Dunno. I sensed a hesitation, an odd chuckle before hanging up. If I didn't know' better—" Bailey's voice trailed off as he chomped down two green Tums.

"Nah, not Dave."

"Trevor was his only child, Moose."

"You know, Jack, another family in Houston will be relieved too."

"I thought of them." Bailey tucked his rumpled shirt into his khaki pants.

—⁜—

Twenty miles away on Houston's west side, Carole and Hal Lewiston read the same article in the *Houston Chronicle*. She called her thirty-year-old daughter-in-law immediately upon finishing.

"Robin, did you see the paper this morning?"

"Carole, you know we don't take the paper."

"Well, brace yourself. Sit down. Bart Bradford was killed in a car accident.

"No shit!"

"It was about ten thirty last night. I'll turn on the TV and see if anything's on."

"OK. I'll call Jay at work and see if he's heard about it." She paused. "At last, retribution for what that scum put Ian and Dad through."

"Yes, finally." Carole's voice was shaky. "I can't believe it. Dad's gonna call Jack Bailey. See what more he can tell us."

—⁜—

Bailey's office was buzzing with activity by ten o'clock. Reporters from the *Herald* and the *Chronicle* hovered outside the door. He fielded phone calls from Mayor Fenn, Captain Murphy, and a Houston cop who had worked the Lewiston case.

Hal Lewiston called immediately after Dave O'Neal.

"Just what the paper said, Hal," Bailey said. "Yeah, I know. Nope, no mention of foul play yet. You bet."

Bailey hung up, and LaGuidas said, "In a few days this'll simmer down." He noted his boss's mood becoming more sour by the minute.

"Right. Then there will be the funeral, more publicity. You'd think the kid was a goddamn Eagle Scout."

"Well, at least Ian and Hal Lewiston are okay now."

"Thank God for that," Bailey mumbled. He remembered hauling Bart Bradford in for his third DUI after killing Trevor O'Neal. Etched in his brain was the smirk the bastard gave him as he walked out the courtroom after the trial, scot free. The kid's perpetual arrogant attitude did nothing for his reputation with the good folks of Richmond, Texas.

—m—

Bailey recalled a bright, warm November day two years ago. Hal and Carole Lewiston, their son, daughter-in-law, and grandson, Ian, drove home from his fourth birthday celebration. As they crossed Westheimer Avenue on a green light, a speeding black Porsche ran a red light and T-boned into the driver's side of the Lewiston car. The other driver, one Bart Bradford II, had a blood alcohol level of .09, and one empty bottle of whiskey was found in the back seat. He sustained minor injuries.

Four-year-old Ian Lewiston wasn't so lucky. The little boy was crushed between his grandparents in the back seat, causing broken ribs and internal injuries. Hal Lewiston underwent three surgeries for fractured limbs and severe head injury. The accident resulted in over a year of hell for the family; medical bills, doctor visits, and physical therapy. Public outrage ensued when Bradford got off with three months in a cushy rehab in California, courtesy of his daddy. His lawyers convinced the jury that .09 alcohol level wasn't high enough to warrant more severe punishment, and at the tender age of twenty-two, he should be given yet another chance.

—m—

Bailey's office was the usual mess when LaGuidas knocked and walked in. Glancing at the piles of junk on the desk, he plopped down in the only uncluttered chair, leaving the door open. "How do you find anything in here?" He knew no answer was forthcoming.

Hector Reyes stepped in with a small box of glazed doughnuts and set it on a stack of files, the only available surface on Bailey's desk. The three men helped themselves and began chomping the treats and sipping stale coffee. LaGuidas brushed crumbs from his neatly pressed polo shirt.

"Hell, it even made the Dallas paper," Bailey growled. "People in the squad are afraid to say anything, but I know we all feel the brat got what he deserved." He gobbled a white Tums to offset the doughnuts.

"Guess we shouldn't play God, but I can't say I wept over it," Reyes said.

A rookie cop knocked on the door with a message for Bailey.

"Captain needs to see you pronto. Sounds serious."

"Crap, now what?" Bailey grumbled.

He walked down the hall and took the stairs at the end. He didn't like being summoned by the captain. For three years they maintained a professional distance because Bailey couldn't stand the guy.

Captain Andrew Murphy was a short sixty-year-old gray haired man who kept in shape by working out at a trendy gym in Houston. One of the few staff members who lived outside the Richmond area, Murphy projected an attitude of urban superiority, Bailey thought. He felt the guy harbored a Napoleon complex; he was boss and made damn sure no one forgot it.

Bailey knocked on the door. He entered when he heard Murphy's, "Come in."

"Have a seat." Murphy waved his hand arrogantly, indicating a leather chair across from his neatly arranged desk. No informalities this morning. Must be serious, Bailey thought. Murphy straightened his red tie on his white collar and looked at Bailey over high end designer reading glasses.

"Something's come up," Murphy said.

"Kinda figured that, since the only time I'm called in here there's trouble."

Murphy ignored the remark and continued, "A couple cops working the Bradford scene came up with some interesting evidence."

"You have my attention. Sometimes evidence is interesting."

"Cut the smart ass attitude, Bailey, and listen. Looks like this wasn't an accident. Our guys found dents on the back passenger side above the wheel and back door, plus—"

"Found dents? You gotta be shittin' me. That car was a heap of scrap metal after the crash. How could they tell anything from that?"

"Let me finish, will you? The area showed the dents were positioned at an angle in the opposite direction of the crumpled fender, plus some other details. It's a mess, but our guy Riley has an eagle eye for this stuff. A Houston forensics guy verified it earlier this morning."

"Oh, well that settles it, a Houston guy. Has to be gospel."

"Look, Bailey, I don't have time for your crap. I'm giving you the short version. You'd be bored stiff listening to the rest. Besides, they also found a few black paint smudges near the dents. Against the navy blue of the kid's Beemer, they almost missed them. And this is the clincher. There were three sets of skid marks along the road. Right alongside the Beemer's. Some of 'em joined Bradford's car on the right side."

"So someone forced the kid off the road, made it look like a one-car?"

"Sure looks that way," Murphy replied.

Bailey had ordered seventy five yards of the road cordoned off around the accident site until the initial investigation was complete. There shouldn't have been car tracks after the accident.

"Everyone knows Bradford had plenty of enemies. More than one person wanted him to get what was coming to him." Bailey refused to think about Dave O'Neal or the Lewiston family.

"I'll keep you posted. Be ready for a homicide investigation. Start thinking about strategy, interviews, all that."

No shit, Bailey thought. Asshole gave him little credit for knowing something about the job.

"Is this public knowledge yet, Murphy?"

"Within the squad, not the press. They'll sniff it out soon enough."

Back in his untidy office, Jack Bailey motioned LaGuidas and Reyes in. He relayed what the captain told him.

LaGuidas cringed. "Damn, now we're stuck with a homicide case."

"Makes sense though," Reyes added. "Think of the people who resent that family."

"Okay, the Cap wants us on it pronto. Moose, let's check out the crime scene again. Hector, ask around, see if you pick up any comments from the cops who worked the scene."

Bailey swallowed a green Tums. He offered the bottle to the other two. They waved it off. "You're the one with the ulcers, Jack," Reyes said.

—m—

An hour later Jack Bailey and Moose LaGuidas walked around the road area examining the pavement. After fifteen minutes, they discerned the skid and track marks Murphy had mentioned.

The demolished car loomed against the tree, still in its resting position. With high power magnifying glasses, the two cops scrutinized the crushed fender and side for evidence of marks and paint. This took longer, but after half an hour, they again discovered everything the captain had informed them of the car's surface.

"Now what," Moose asked, "as if I didn't know."

"Look at the evidence. Get our guys to try and match the tires and car paint. Guess I'll check the alibis."

"Gonna start with O'Neal?"

"Yeah, his son's the only fatality caused by the little scum. Then the Lewistons.

A couple other vics got their cars wrecked, but no injuries. Forgot their names so I'll look 'em up."

—⁂—

Three days later, Jack Bailey had talked with Dave O'Neal, and his wife, Susy, along with the Lewiston family. Hal and Carole had not seemed shocked that the accident morphed to a homicide. Jay and Robin, their son and daughter-in-law, seemed the most surprised of anyone. Bailey chalked it up to naiveté of the younger generation.

Bailey admitted to himself that of the people he interviewed, the O'Neals had been the least surprised at the news. In fact, Dave O'Neal had been downright smug about it. All parties, however, had indisputable alibis. No surprise to Bailey.

—⁂—

One week later, he, LaGuidas, and Reyes commiserated about the Bradford case in Bailey's office. They drank coffee and chomped cardboard cinnamon rolls. Bailey brushed crumbs from his shirt onto the floor.

"Looks like a cold case," Reyes said.

"Yeah, people don't give a damn. Except the Bradfords, of course," LaGuidas said.

Bailey shrugged. "With no way to locate flimsy paint chip and tire track leads, that's about it. Bradford and his kid had too many enemies to start questioning all of them."

—⁂—

Ten days later, Captain Murphy knocked on Bailey's office door and opened it.

"Come right in," Bailey said flippantly after Murphy sat down.

"Got news on the Bradford case. Closed until further notice."

"I'm shocked." Bailey feigned surprise.

"Too many loose ends to spend more department time and money on it. If old man Bradford wants to hire his own investigators, fine. I've had it."

Bailey had a new respect for the man. "I agree, Murph. We're on the same page."

"Have a good one, Jack," Murphy said as he got up to leave. He looked around. "And straighten up this place."

Moose LaGuidas came in on Murphy's heels. He closed the door, a strange expression on his face.

"What?" Bailey asked.

"One of the guys from the Bradford scene came up to me just now. He'd been out yesterday after hours for one last look. A few yards from the wreck, his dog was sniffing and pawing at something." LaGuidas cleared his throat. "The pooch found a dead bird. Something was partially hidden under it. He looked closer and picked up the item. Brought it in and showed it to me." LaGuidas stared at his friend. The clock on the wall ticked off the seconds as silence thickened the air.

"Well, what the hell did he find?" Bailey demanded.

"An empty packet of Tums."

—⚜— WHEN TO CALL 911 —⚜—

Jim Murtha

FRANK ORDERED HIS THIRD boilermaker and offered to buy me one. I declined, content to sip my light beer. He was his usual self-centered son-of-a-bitch self, growing loud and checking the clock frequently. He drained his half-empty beer glass, slid it and the empty shot glass to the ledge on the back of the bar, and looked my way. "How's your kid doing with football this year? Any of the old man's talents?"

"Buddy made the team, but there're two guys ahead of him at flanker. One of them lettered the last two years. With luck, Buddy'll play enough to make the practice worth it."

He nodded then said, "How's Cheryl? Still into yoga? I bet she's hot in those Capris. It amazes me she chose you when she could have her pick from the god-damned graduating class."

I tolerated Frank's taunts. I was accustomed to his style. Besides, he was my boss. "Cheryl's fine, busy with the girls' activities, doing volunteer work at their school. And still doing yoga. Did you want to talk anymore about the Wilkins project, Frank?"

"Nah, just an excuse to have a couple of drinks with my favorite tech guy. You gave me all I need to know in the first twenty minutes. Just write it up the way I told you. I've wanted to get even with that bastard Wilkins and here's my chance. This is my last drink. I'm just killing time now. I've got a little action waiting: a real nympho, and a little nutty."

I glanced at him. "How's Kitty these days?"

Frank shot me a mean look, then turned it into a grin. "Kitty is Kitty. Always and ever. Same old, same old. Up at her mother's the rest of the week." He signaled for our tab, then laughed loud enough for the whole bar to hear. "When the Kitty's away, the mouse will play."

I stared at my beer, rotating the glass, knowing no one here knew us, but I was embarrassed nonetheless. We came here once before, several months before. It was a little out of the way. People minded their own business and it was quiet: no pool table, no juke box, with one TV at the opposite end of the bar.

It wasn't the first time Frank bragged to me about his conquests. I wondered if he told other guys at work. As far as I knew, I was the only one who knew Kitty.

Frank downed his shot and chased it with half a glass of beer. "Don't look so shocked. You're so goddamned naïve. I bet we took a poll here, ninety percent of these guys would say they get a little on the side. Even you're not perfect, as I recall. What was the name of that broad in Phoenix? You remember her, don't you, Alec? Oh yeah—Wanda."

I wasn't anxious to pursue the subject. I reached for the tab. "Let me get the drinks."

Frank grabbed the tab, glanced at it, peeled three twenties from his clip, and tossed them onto the bar. "My party, kid. You get the next one. Time for me to seize the day. That's the difference between us, pal. I'm your boss 'cause I know how to handle opportunity when I see it. You gotta grab it by the balls, which is something this chick likes to do."

While Frank laughed at his joke, we collected our jackets and headed out the back door into the parking lot.

Frank eased into his silver BMW as I started my Prius and turned on the lights. I was surprised at how dark it was, and then remembered we had returned to standard time over the weekend.

I drove out ahead of Frank. Rush hour traffic had died down. During the short drive to the highway, I called Cheryl. While we talked, Frank passed, honking his horn and making a gesture I didn't understand. Cheryl reminded me that she and the girls were going to a ballet recital at the school and Buddy was staying at a friend's house. There were leftovers from the night before and frozen guacamole.

It was a pleasant drive in the daytime—rolling hills, pastures with dairy cattle, and the occasional cluster of houses. Both Frank and I lived in Somerset, a village of older homes on large lots in a river valley barely visible from the highway, far enough away that you couldn't hear the traffic. The office commute was forty-five minutes door to door, but worth it to be out of the dreary din of the city.

Who was Frank's heavy date? I hoped not someone from work. While he had a reputation for making inappropriate comments to women, I'd never heard of any groping, much less liaisons. I was surprised he brought up that Phoenix business trip. I felt horrible afterward and nearly told Cheryl about it.

I slid Dvorak's cello concerto into my CD player and set the cruise control, trying to get my mind off the scene at the bar. Stars began to appear. No moon yet. Traffic was light in both directions. I slowed as I approached Wadley, the halfway point of the trip, getting stuck as usual at the solitary stop light. In the next block, I saw Frank pull out of a parking lot next to a bank. Someone in the passenger seat tossed a beer can out the window. Must be the nympho. Where were they headed? There were no motels along this stretch.

No sign of Frank's car the rest of the way to Somerset. I drove up my lane and into the garage, where I listened to the final minutes of the concerto before going into the house.

I took the leftovers from the fridge, put two pots on the stove to reheat, thawed the guacamole, and poured a glass of Syrah. I changed into jeans and a sweat shirt and spent the next hour or so at my desk, eating, checking email, and editing a report on the Wilkins project, based on Frank's comments. I'd just loaded the dishwasher when the phone rang. The caller ID indicated Frank's home phone.

"Hey, Frank, what's up?"

"Why didn't you answer your cell, Alec? I left two messages. I didn't want to call you at home in case Cheryl answered." His breath came in gulps. I could imagine his clenched jaw.

"Sorry, must've left the phone in the car. Cheryl and the kids are out for the evening. What's going on?"

"I need your help. Can you come over now?"

"Can't this wait until morning?"

Frank yelled, "I need you now!"

"Can you at least tell me what it is?"

"No. Just get your ass over here. And bring some work gloves." He hung up.

I collected my keys and billfold, locked up the house, grabbed some garden gloves in the garage, and headed out. Calling Cheryl could wait until I had a better idea of what was going on. Frank sounded desperate. Had he taken that woman to his house? What the hell were the gloves about? Was I going to carry something dirty?

The drive took five minutes. I pulled up the driveway, past the oversized flag flapping in the breeze, past the turnaround with Frank's trailered powerboat, past the Grecian water fountain, and parked outside the triple-car garage. The side door next to the garage was ajar, so I went in. Frank sat at the bottom of the wooden stairway. His face was flushed. Sweat ran down his forehead.

"Been a horrible accident. That chick is in my bedroom. Dead." Same strained voice as on the phone. His bloodshot eyes begged me to understand. His bulky shoulders sagged. His hands hung between his knees.

"What kind of accident?" I said. "Did she fall?" For an instant, I wondered if this was one of Frank's practical jokes.

"She wanted to do this goofy thing. She wanted me to strangle her until she almost passes out. Supposed to make better sex. She passed out. Never came to."

"You sure she's dead?"

"See for yourself, pal." He trudged up the stairs.

I stood at the bottom. Half of me didn't want to see, but I had to.

I climbed the polished oak stairs and followed him to the master bedroom. A naked woman lay face up on the floor, bruises on her neck and cheeks, mouth agape, staring at the ceiling. On the bed, a red scarf rested on a wet pillow. I kneeled down. The body was warm, her skin soft. Her bloodshot eyes bulged. A strand of matted sweat drenched hair was caught on the clumped ebony mascara smeared across her cheek. Maybe she was a looker an hour ago, but now she projected terror and vulnerability. There was no pulse.

"Frank, how long ago did this happen?" my voice shrill with panic and fists clenched at my temples.

"Maybe ten minutes before I called you. I slapped her, yelled at her. Threw water on her face."

"Did you try mouth-to-mouth?"

"No. I don't know how. But she was gone. I unloaded my trunk space, thinking I could get rid of her body, but dragging her off the bed, I knew I couldn't do it alone."

I stared at the body, and imagined dumping her in a trash container or a shallow grave. I felt like I was in a movie. I smelled pot. I looked around the room again, spotting a bottle of brandy and two glasses on the side table. I looked up at Frank. "Gotta call 911. Now. Even if they can't help, we gotta call."

"Bullshit! They'll think I killed her. I can't have this slut dead in my house. You need to help me get rid of the body."

"Can't do that, Frank. They'll track you down."

"No one knows about us. I met her at a bar a month ago; we went to a motel room by the interstate. Separate cars. No one saw her come or go. This is only the second time I've seen her; she called my disposable phone out of the blue. She's dead now, for Christ's sake. Nothing we do will change that."

"Frank, listen—"

"No, you listen, motherfucker! I'm not going to ruin my life letting the cops come. My only mistake was bringing her here. I wanted an all-nighter. Was gonna drop her off on the way to work. She left her car in Wadley, but she lives in the city."

"Frank, this is crazy. She's not the first person to die trying this suffocation stuff. Let the police handle it. Tell them it was an accident."

Frank grabbed my shoulders and shoved his face close to mine. "Not in a million years. Think what it would do to my reputation, to Kitty. I'd lose my job. I couldn't face my neighbors. We'll ditch her body somewhere off the highway. No one will ever trace her to me."

"What about her car? The cops will suspect she was heading out this way to meet someone," I said, buying time, hoping to dissuade him.

"We'll ditch her and her car. I've got a place in mind. Another reason I need your help."

I shook my head. "You're my boss, but I can't afford to risk my life covering up an accidental death. I'm willing to tell the cops you called me to help revive her because I know CPR. That'll substantiate your story that her death was an accident."

"Don't you understand, Alec? I am not calling the cops. I'd be ruined even if they believed it was an accident. Either you're with me on this or you're not."

"Sorry, Frank. So far, I haven't committed a crime. But if I help you hide the body, that's a crime."

"You asshole! We won't get caught. It'll be over in a couple of hours. Tell Cheryl I called you to meet a client who showed up unexpectedly."

"I'm leaving now, Frank."

Frank stared at me and smiled. "Before you leave, Alec, think about our trip to Phoenix."

The menace in his voice immobilized me. "We agreed to bury that, Frank. We both did things we weren't proud of. Fortunately no one got hurt, and I learned my lesson."

"Right, no one was hurt, but you made a fool of yourself with Wanda in the backseat of the rental. She probably remembers more than we do, because she didn't drink much. Too busy pleasing my pal Alec, the guy who told her he'd just got divorced. What's Cheryl and your kids gonna think?"

I took a deep breath. I'd cheated on Cheryl once, when the kids were young. My conscience wouldn't let me forget it, so I'd confessed to her. It took us months to get over it. She said she'd make my life miserable if it happened again. And how could I face the kids, especially Buddy, who thought I walked on water. "What's your plan, Frank? I'm not saying I'll help, but I'll listen."

"That's my boy, Alec. We get our gloves, carry her down the stairs, and put her in my trunk. We drive back to her car. You drive her car and follow me.

There's a turnoff just outside of Wadley that dead-ends at Jones Creek. We put her into her front seat then push the car over the bank into the water. She's had plenty of booze already. It'll look like an accident."

"Sounds pretty flimsy. Besides, it'll take a long time."

"Twenty minutes to Wadley, another twenty getting rid of the car, and twenty minutes back here. Twenty more for good measure. You'll be back at your house in less than an hour and a half. Leave a message for Cheryl saying I asked you to bring some work here to review."

"What if I say no, Frank? Then you can't get rid of both the body and the car. Besides, your car isn't exactly inconspicuous. People would remember seeing it."

"I've got a backup plan, Alec. There's another guy I could call to come and help. I'd have to pay him, but he wouldn't care about the chick. He'd enjoy dumping her and the car into the creek. Then I'd make your life miserable both at work and with your family. You're up a shit creek, like it or not."

I wondered if he was bluffing. Could I explain Phoenix to Cheryl after such a long time? Would Frank find a way to implicate me if I walked away now or later if he was caught?

I stared at the floor and considered my options. My former office mate Jason came to mind. Once he contradicted Frank in a meeting with a client. Frank not only fired him, but he made sure Jason never got past a first interview with any of our competition. Eventually, Jason switched careers. Frank rose in the ranks by walking over people to get what he wanted, regardless of how others got hurt. He was a real prick. Shaking my head slowly, I said, "Okay."

We both went down and got our gloves. Frank pulled on a pair of work boots. When we returned, Frank said, "You grab her legs and I'll get the other end. Let me go down first. Be damn careful when we get to the stairs."

We worked the corpse down the hall to the top of the stairs and stopped for a breath. Frank took two steps down and turned around. He slid his arms under the woman's armpits and pulled her close to his chest. "Lift her legs and kinda pull back, so I can work my way down without all the weight."

Frank lifted the body and took another step. I held back, so Frank had to lean backwards to maintain his balance. When he took the next step, I lifted her legs quickly and pushed hard, forcing her body down onto Frank. He fell backward. His head banged against the hand rail then smacked on the stairs. The momentum carried him and the body tumbling down into a tangle at the bottom.

I stood there waiting for movement, but there was none. I walked down the stairs and stepped over the bodies. Frank's head was at a funny angle and blood pooled underneath. I removed one glove and checked several places on Frank's neck for a pulse. Nothing. Good. I was ready to finish the job if necessary.

I reviewed my movements, then walked back up the stairs, surveyed the scene in the bedroom, and used a tissue to wipe any surface I might have touched.

I went out to my car and checked my cell phone. There were two messages from Frank, both saying, "Alec, call me immediately." I'd been there fifteen minutes. How could I account for that time? I'd just have to say I hadn't left my house immediately after Frank called. No one had a record of the panicked conversation on my home phone, so the only evidence would be the times the calls were placed.

I stared down at my phone and punched in a number.

"911. What is your emergency?"

"My friend's dead. And there's a woman I don't know. She's dead, too. I need the police."

—ᴡ— STORM RUNNER —ᴡ—

Rob Hunsaker

ONE DAY IN A neighborhood where all of the houses were alike, where all of the people who could be seen looked alike and of those who spoke, spoke alike, lived a man and his family. The man and his wife worked hard every day and took care of their suburban house and their daughter took care to make good grades in school. All was well in their little house; however, money was tight and time was tighter and the bill collector and the tax man were closing in on them. Subsequently, everyone in the house was uncomfortable and worried most of the time.

One evening, right before dark, a terrible storm began to blow in from the north. The skies darkened over the setting sun, the birds went to wherever they go when they are not flying, and the lightning filled the sky and frightened most men and creatures alike. When the rain came, it was driven by the wind and crashed down in raging horizontal sheets. The family huddled in the living room and the mother reassured her daughter and reassured her husband and silently reassured herself that all was going to be all right. They believed her yet were still anxious. And so they sat and waited in silence.

The man, whose senses were on alert, thought he heard a scratching at the front door. He went to the door and barely cracked it open to find a long haired, bobbed tail cat, soaking wet and calmly sitting on his haunches. The cat looked up at him and let out a single meow. He opened the door all the way and the little cat casually walked into the house.

Once inside the house, the mother got a towel to dry him off; the daughter poured him a saucer of milk, and the man petted him. Eventually, the winds died down and the rain stopped and soon the long haired, short tailed, grey and white cat became a beloved member of the household. The mother named him Archie and the man and the daughter agreed that it was a good name and began to call him Archie as well.

After Archie's arrival, the fortunes of the house began to change. The man got a promotion at his job; the daughter began getting straight "A's" on her report card, and the woman didn't have to clean the house as much as she used to. In fact, the man made so much money now that his wife didn't have to work anymore and everyone was happy.

A few months after Archie arrived at their door, a storm began brewing outside and over the little neighborhood. Before the rain started, Archie began scratching at the door wanting to get out. The man opened the door for him and he ran out of the house and down the street running in the direction of the wind. The storm came and eventually left. As the water cleared, the family went out looking for Archie, their beloved cat. They looked everywhere up and down every street within a few miles. The family eventually gave up and went home. The mother made hot chocolate for her family and everyone was sad for a few days.

Life went on for the family and, in slow order; their spirits began to lift as Archie faded into a pleasant memory for them. The family's fortunes were still high and their lives together were happy. A few weeks after Archie left, the man was on his way home from work and he noticed a new luxury car in the driveway of one of the houses a few blocks from his. He slowed down to admire the car and noticed Archie sitting in the front window of the house. He stopped in front of the house, rolled down his window and looked at Archie. Archie and the man looked at each other from across the yard. They both smiled and Archie winked at the man. Noticing that the cat appeared to be healthy and happy the man rolled up his window and drove home.

He talked to his family about seeing Archie, and they all agreed to let him stay with the other family. From that day on, the man noticed the house where Archie was staying started to look better kept, like his did. He noticed the yard was getting greener and the shrubs had been sculptured into beautiful animal shapes. A week later the windows had new curtains and two weeks later the house got a new roof.

This went on for the whole summer, but one day on a Saturday in the early fall, a terrible storm began brewing on the horizon and was descending on the little neighborhood from the north. The man and his family were on their way home from a charity auction and were anxious to get home before the storm. They were stopped at the stop sign a few blocks from their house and amongst the lighting and running with the wind, they saw Archie running down the sidewalk in a frenzied flash.

The rain began and he suddenly ran over to the front door of the closest house to him. The man and his family watched in awe as Archie began scratching at the front door of the house. The door stayed shut and the wind began to pick up. The car began to shake and the door of the house began to bow inward. The man and his family were frightened but became petrified at the next sight.

The clouds formed a funnel that dipped down from the sky, and with surgical precision, lapped at the front door of the house until it blew wide open. Then as fast as it came, the clouds parted, the winds died down and there was nothing left but a gentle light rain. Archie arose and slowly walked inside the house and sidled up to a sad, frightened, yet excited young boy with braces on his legs.

—ɯ— BOWL OF CHERRIES (MIXED MEDIA) —ɯ—

AC Rogers

BEWARE OF FEDERICO ALFONSO. He exposes your deepest secrets to the oxidizing air, then sets you loose. She should have known better, with her pretty ears and creamy skin, should have abandoned her decorum and run away before he unrolled his brushes.

And then, without him, without her, I wouldn't exist. And you would not have come here today, as others have, for decades now. You stand in front of me and it begins. At first, your arms are crossed, as if a closed posture could armour you. The line of your jaw tells me you are determined to be clinical, technical; you move close enough to see the brushwork, nose twitching as if the vibrancy of my paint were fresh, then further back to view the overall effect. At first you see nothing special, only the marbling where, over the years, my ingredients have separated slightly. you are disappointed, and this chink of emotion begins your undoing. You relax a little. Arms fall by your sides, a finger reaches up to tap your lips, searching, wondering. Why have so many people come to view me? Why are there so many stories about the madness that follows? Certainly the reprints have no such effect. Is it something in the air around me? A pathogen given off by the mixed media he is famous for?

Many have studied this; men and women with frames around their eyes, white,drubberized hands, have taken air samples, even desecrated a small piece of the canvas top right, where most people do not look. You know they found nothing. I appear as all the other paintings, more or less. And so the mystery persists, and people come. And they go. And some of them meet a violent, self-inflicted death.

The air around you and inside you churns with all that you do not know, with all that you wish to know. Why is a still life, a plain white bowl of deep red cherries, hanging in the portrait section of the gallery? Why did the artist insist upon it,—famous as he is, he retains that kind of power, even now. Was it merely a publicity stunt, to get the world talking? But now that they are talking, how do you explain the other effects? And why is there one cherry, suspended by its stalk, falling out of the bowl? Your hand hovers: you, too, wish to put it back. Not even I am sure how he achieved that effect.

Ah, now they start, youerealize you've opened yourself. You peer at the luscious fruit, the thick globs of paint and whatever else he incorporated. They morph out of the canvas, swollen sirens to the tactile and you feel a kick low down in the belly. Your pupils dilate, saliva deserts you, and gradually every hair follicle rises up,dmagnetized. The blood begins to hammer at your throat, demanding attention, longing for touch. Your tongue peeps at your lips, you shift closer to me and breathe in something you know wasn't there before. Like a scent passing an open window: a single molecule enough to trigger primitive aware-ness, though not identification.

Your hands shimmer—not vigorously, not a tremor—but you are unnerved. You glance behind you, half afraid the feelings will go when you turn back. How-ever, I am not inconsiderate, and when your eyes caress me again, you know the agony of delayed gratification. Except there can be no gratification, only the wait, the wait for something impossible. You want to possess me, yet you don't mean to hang me on a wall. I am not about that kind of possession, there is no owner-ship here.

You want to be enveloped, to drown, to give yourself up to an inundation of ecstasy, the dissolving of yourself. And then down falls hopelessness. You under-stand. How can you make love to a painting? For this is what you long for. There is lust, for sure, but you don't just want a good fuck, this is something more spiritual, there is a connection you feel, however crazy that sounds. A piece of canvas in a heavy wooden frame! The balloon of lust and longing inflates inside you, choking off sensation and blood to your other organs. You are smothered by it. By the impossibility of this desire for something so implausible. Not just out of reach. You don't risk death by making love to me, it is simply beyond the laws of physics.

Briefly, you ponder that. What if? What if you steal me and lie with me on a bed? Clothed? Unclothed?

No! You break away, walk resolutely out of the room, hand tugging at the roots of your hair as if I can be so easily ripped out. I let you go. I know you will return.

—m—

What you feel is nothing. Nothing to the maelstrom of when he made me. When they made me, I was supposed to be a formal portrait. Something for the mantelpiece, for her husband to call property in a way he deigned this not to her face. Though she was his. They were the kind of people who wore clothes easily, yet were weighted as if the safety of nations rested on their shoulders. Perhaps it did—I know nothing outside his studio, and this gallery.

I've learned the interiors of people. Federico taught me that. How the body talks of fear and lust soundlessly—for, without hearing, I have no use for words. That opening and closing of mouths, the churning of tongues which people need to interpret, or misread. I watched him translate character onto canvas, and since then, I have seen most types of people parade before me; waited for their neuroses to leech through their clothe, into the air between us.

When she came into the room, she brought with her a tornado. Or they created it between them, like blue and yellow making green. I've seen the sky glow green when enough warm moist air meets a cold jet stream blast. They mingle, shear and begin to twist, creating a force that nothing manmade can withstand, much less contain. The resulting windstorm is unpredictable and destructive. Green is also the colour of jealousy, which perhaps you already know from experience.

That day he perspired freely, removed his shirt, opened the window onto the frost-covered world outside. But it made no difference. Their collision was inevitable. For a month they did not touch. He sketched and painted, offered her sustenance: grapes or cherries, sometimes strawberries. Agitated by the syncopated rhythm from the bar beneath his studio, he made four portraits, from which she smiled benignly, regally. And he hated them all.

When he reached for my prepared surface, his warm fingertips caressing my frame, I believe we both trembled. Perhaps he didn't yet know what he was about to create. The Wizard in thrall to his Muse. He placed his hands, damp with anticipation, gently on my topmost edge. With a light touch, he brushed his fingers from top to bottom, sensing the quality of my canvas, feeling the space for the image he would bring out, like a sculptor, from my uniform cream. He leaned forward and placed his burning forehead to my cool, rough surface.

Everything that touched me I absorbed. Saliva from the gnawed pencil that scratched my form, his breath, sweat, paint, whatever he held I took. The cherries themselves, cut by her teeth, touched by her lips before he crushed them onto the drying globs of paint. Rounding them with a knife, including the magenta drops of his own cut finger to render the shadow inside the bowl just so.

The colours and chemicals burned themselves into me until I embodied the surging hunger of the pair before me. While his eyes were on me, creating, our mutual pain faded a little.; I helped draw it from him, like a poison. Then he would look to her again and the longing returned. I ached until his eyes caressed me. I don't care what you believe about the clichés of artists: the horny satyrs, using sitters and models like rags for their brushes. He was not like that. She was the only one.

On the day they finally collided, I was almost complete, and the other portraits had cured. He abandoned me high on the easel and wound the gramophone when he reached for her. I watched as they touched, swayed and tangled each other up on the coat strewn floor of the studio. It was then that the bitterness of longing, of impossibility, hardened in me with the paint. And with every passing year, it matures and strengthens, a grande cuvée.

I was covered up, of course, on the day her husband came to choose his favorites among the portraits. And after they left, arms linked, he held me once more, his thumb softly stroking the shapes he had created. He allowed one tear to drop to my canvas, where it half sank in, half dried up. I am the proof of his passion, of her infidelity, even if they are the only two who can express it in words.

—⁂—

Ah, you have come back to me. And you have diminished once more. When you come close, I see the hairs, growing mismatched and careless, on your chin line, ignored by the razor. You do not inhabit your clothes anymore, they overwhelm you. You breathe me in, searching once more for the high, the swooping dizziness to envelope you. Then you step back, heart freight-training. The high is diminished too, the pit of despair deepened.

Then they come for you. The men and women in official blue uniforms. They are alert to this now. To people who return again and again to gaze at me, to the desperation that trails after them like a surreptitious odor. You look right and left, and they hold your arms gently, steer you away from me, mouths moving as if words of advice will take away the pain. And I know that soon a group of them will stand around me and wave their arms, arguing about my continued presence, the guilt they feel, the inexplicability of it all.

But I think I will stay a while longer. Even at the zenith of his influence, her husband dared not remove me. As if by acknowledging me, he would have been complicit in his own downfall. On the day he viewed me with a delegation, with her by his side, pretending I was merely oil on canvas, he knew. As if the scent of Federico's studio, years earlier, had survived in me to betray her. He saw her change in my presence. Like an exotic insect shedding its dowdy chrysalis, her decorum dropped away and once more her skin glowed, her breathing deep and fragrant. When she reached up to touch me, I burned. He knew it, and so did everyone with him.

Such was the power of Federico's alchemy. Yet even he was not immune to what he had unleashed. He, too, was drawn to me as he diminished, each time thinner and more savage than before. He tried painting me again, brought easel and brushes and copied me, in many colours, in monochrome, as if the act could save him. In the end he stood in front of me one darkened evening, lips moving silently. I watched the pulse at his temple, at his throat, leaping as a caged animal longing for escape. Finally, before they noticed, he removed the revolver from his bulky overcoat and raised it with a quivering hand.

—ᴗ— CONTRIBUTORS —ᴗ—

ANDREA BARBOSA is an award-winning novelist and poet, and currently maintains an Indie review blog. *Massive Black Hole—Cibele's Hell*, her contemporary women's novel, is listed as one of the 50 Self Published Books Worth Reading for 2013/2014 (reader voted top 5 in literary fiction) at ReadFree.ly. Her poetry collection, *Holes in Space*, received a 5 star seal and the 2015 Silver Medal Award in Poetry from Readers' Favorite, and is featured in the 50 Best Books of 2014 at ReadFree.ly, voted top 5 in poetry by readers. Her short story, "The Match" features on the Eclectically Criminal anthology, by Inklings Publishing. She has received an Honorable Mention Award for her flash fiction in the 2015 Spider's Web Flash Fiction Contest from Spider Road Press. For more of her writing, follow her: Blog: http://massive-blackholenovel.blogspot.com. Follow her on twitter at: @andyb0810

Born and raised in Bryan, Texas, ELIZABETH DOMINO enrolled in a Creative Writing class in Fall of 2007 with Dr. Joe Aimone. Attending for the sake of fulfilling a requisite for an English credit for her Art degree, she found that he opened her heart and mind to writing. And ultimately herself. She became addicted to writing, writing workshops and critique groups and in the spring of 2009 contributed four short stories to the on campus publication, *The Bayou Review*. Upon leaving school she maintained her writing of short stories as well as an online blog entitled *Ramblings of an Ovary* and then became a staff writer to a lifestyle magazine, *Act Badd*, in 2012 until January of 2014. She currently contributes short story fiction and poetry to another blog, *Curators of Dopeness* every Tuesday while maintaining the grind of her legitimate 9-5 job that keeps her children fed and her lights on and water running.

H.R HUNSAKER was born in Oklahoma City. Raised in Conroe Texas from the age of 5 and moved to the big city in his 20's. A middle aged factory worker, Rob is captivated by Houston and is still awestruck by the enormity of the downtown buildings and the diversity of the city. Rob went to college in is late 30's and graduated from the University of Houston-Downtown with a BA in English. Rob is a part time author of short fiction and one, yet to be published, novel: *Across From the Bayou*. Rob's fiction tends to gravitate towards the working man and his struggles in adapting to changing and failed social systems. When he is motivated, Rob adds stories to his Facebook page *Working Title: Unknown* by H.R. Hunsaker. Here you can find his experimental audio cartoon *The Adventures of Cowboy Jessie and Cowboy Earl*. The author currently lives in North Houston with his one and only ex-wife; they both believe in second chances.

Born near Pittsburgh, Pennsylvania, JOYCE KOPP has migrated westward and southward. Currently a member of The Woodlands Writers Guild in Texas, she is learning about writing short stories and working on a novella. However, her first love as a teenager was poetry. In October 2013, she had her first short story published in *Affaire de Coeur* magazine. In 2014, two short stories appeared in *Aspiring Writers 2014 Winners Anthology*; in 2015, one in *A Quick Read: One Minute Stories from Around the World*. In January 2014, she had her first poem, "In deference to negligence," published in *Northern Liberties Review*. She is honored to have published in 2015, "Uninvited," in the anthology *Candles of Hope: A Collection of Cancer Poetry*, GWL Publishing, UK.

MEG LELVIS grew up in northern Minnesota, and has lived in Texas for over 30 years. She taught English and psychology for 17 years, and now lives in Houston with her husband and two dogs.

MARY JO MARTIN is an award-winning writer who gave up life inside the loop and now lives in the suburbs of Houston, Texas. She is a member of the Houston Writer's Guild. A personal medical mystery led her to pen an account of her quest to find her father's medical history. Instead, she discovered a huge family. This work won first place in the memoir category in a Houston Writer's Guild contest. Mary Jo started her professional life as a chemist. Along the way, she sold out to the dark side, got an MBA, and practiced marketing and market research for forty years. After years of doing concise business writing, she is now free to do "real" writing.

JIM MURTHA retired in 2013 from a technical career, mathematics and engineering, to devote his time to writing fiction and memoirs, which he did secretly most of his life.

PATRICIA FLAHERTY PAGAN grew up near Boston, and spent a summer working at a farm stand. She thought getting her MFA in creative writing from Goddard College was hard, until she tried adopting two Indonesian street cats. She founded Spider Road Press to publish writing by and/or about strong women. Her fiction collection, *Trail Ways Pilgrims: Stories*, which features the award-winning story "Bargaining," was published in 2015. Her short fiction and essays have been published in several journals and anthologies, including *Tides of Impossibility, Our Space: Poetry and Shorts from the Houston Community, Fierce with Reality*, and *Eve's Requiem: Tales of Women, Mystery, and Horror*. When not writing, she hikes and travels with the world's most patient husband.

AC ROGERS writes short stories and novels. She was born in South Africa, grew up in the UK, and continues to travel and live where work and blind chance take her. She wrote her first stories as a child, and after some years of dabbling in other ideas, learning Spanish, and being distracted by jobs that paid her to travel, finally got around to taking an MA in Creative Writing from Manchester Metropolitan University. A keen amateur sailor, she has cruised and raced in Europe, USA and more exotic places. Although a contented city dweller for many years, she has a secret yearning for wild places and empty horizons that sometimes leak into the stories she writes. She currently lives in Houston, Texas, with her husband and two children.

VERSTANDT R. A. SHELTON is Inklings Publishing's cover artist. Growing up as a childhood misfit, Verstandt wiled away the hours daydreaming of floating in space and sitting at the bottom of the ocean floor. A disquieting obsession for the less beaten paths of philosophical ponderings and environmental extremes led him to stumble into the murky depths of the writerly craft. You can find him today chained in the back of his closet, with the lights out, a bottle of whiskey in hand, and the ghosts of his inspirations (Stephen King, Clive Barker, Milton, Lovecraft, and Dante) breathing down his neck, writing stories to terrify the world. His lovely wife, Jennifer, and his cat Siouxsie Q worry for his safety.

TERESA TRENT is a cozy mystery writer and is the author of the *Pecan Bayou* Mystery Series. Teresa received a degree in English from University of Northern Colorado and loves to write every day. The story she submitted for this anthology is different from her cozy mysteries, but after years of watching "Twilight Zone" and listening to "Suspense" on old time radio podcasts, she wanted to dive into something a little less Mayberry. Teresa lives in Houston with her family and fills her time with writing, teaching and taking care of her adult son with Down syndrome.

DAVID WELLING is a Houston-based writer, artist, and graphic designer. His lifelong interest in movies (and the places that show them) led to the writing of *Cinema Houston: From Nickelodeon to Megaplex*, which chronicles the history of movie theatres in Texas' largest city. *Cinema Houston* is the recipient of the 2008 Julia Ideson Award from the Friends of the Texas Room, and the Society of Architectural Historians' 2009 Antoinette Forrester Downing Award. He is now writing fiction. His website and blog is davidwelling.com.

About the Houston Writers Guild

THE HOUSTON WRITERS GUILD is a community of writers of all skill levels striving to improve their craft and career through education and camaraderie.

The Guild was founded in 1998 by Roger Paulding with seven participants and has grown to more than 200 active members today. Over its first fifteen years, the Guild sponsored 36 workshops and six 2-day conferences. Roger led the group until 2013, when he passed the reins to Pamela Fagan Hutchins. On September 17, 2014, after a terrific year of leadership, Pamela passed the torch on to Fernanda Brady and Denise Satterfield. Together they are geared up to take HWG to a higher level. Their vision is, with the help of volunteers, to make the Houston Writers Guild a household name in the writing community.

The Guild offers its members workshops/conferences/webinars to learn about their craft and critique groups with excellent participant feedback. It creates opportunities to build careers through networking, as well as, opportunities for author book sales throughout the Greater Houston area and neighboring communities.

Houston Writers Guild
houstonwritersguild.org
P.O.Box 42255
Houston, TX 77242